BY ZOE WHITTALL

FICTION

The Fake

The Spectacular

The Best Kind of People

The Middle Ground

Holding Still for as Long as Possible

Bottle Rocket Hearts

POETRY

Precordial Thump

The Emily Valentine Poems

The Best Ten Minutes of Your Life

WILD
FAILURE

WILD FAILURE

Stories

ZOE WHITTALL

BALLANTINE BOOKS

NEW YORK

A Ballantine Books Trade Paperback Original

Published in the United States by Ballantine Books, an imprint of Random House, a division of Penguin Random House LLC, New York.

BALLANTINE BOOKS & colophon are registered trademarks of Penguin Random House LLC.

Originally published in hardcover in Canada by HarperCollins Publishers Ltd, in 2024.

Portions of this work originally appeared, sometimes in different form, in *Hazlitt*, *Granta*, and *Maisonneuve*. An early version of "A Patch of Bright Flowers" appeared in *Persistence: All Ways Butch and Femme*, edited by Ivan Coyote and Zena Sharman (Vancouver, BC: Arsenal Pulp Press, 2011), and "The Sex Castle Lunch Buffet" in *Sluts* edited by Michelle Tea (Los Angeles: Dopamine Books, 2024).

Library of Congress Cataloging-in-Publication Data
Names: Whittall, Zoe, author.
Title: Wild failure: stories / Zoe Whittall.
Description: New York: Ballantine Books, 2024.
Identifiers: LCCN 2024004285 (print) | LCCN 2024004286 (ebook) | ISBN 9780593499917 (trade paperback) | ISBN 9780593499924 (ebook)
Subjects: LCSH: Women—Fiction. | LCGFT: Short stories.
Classification: LCC PR9199.4.W48 W55 2024 (print) | LCC PR9199.4.W48 (ebook) | DDC 813/.6—dc23/eng/20240202
LC record available at https://lccn.loc.gov/2024004285
LC ebook record available at https://lccn.loc.gov/2024004286

Printed in the United States of America on acid-free paper

randomhousebooks.com

2 4 6 8 9 7 5 3 1

Book design by Caroline Cunningham
Title page background: Adobe Stock/孤飞的鹤
Title page floral illustrations: Adobe Stock/Hulinska Yevheniia

For Team Jawlz

My femininity is about irony. It is a statement about the construction of gender; it is not just an appropriation of gender. It is not being a girl, it is watching yourself be a girl.

—AMBER HOLLIBAUGH, *My Dangerous Desires*

The Sex Wars are over, I've been told, and it always makes me want to ask who won.

—DOROTHY ALLISON, *Skin: Talking About Sex, Class, and Literature*

CONTENTS

HALF-PIPE   3

WILD FAILURE   25

MORE HOLY   41

OH, EL   55

A PATCH OF BRIGHT FLOWERS   69

THIS IS CARRIE'S WHOLE LIFE   87

THE SEX CASTLE LUNCH BUFFET   99

I NEED A MIRACLE   115

I'M STILL YOUR FAG   133

MURDER AT THE ELM STREET
COLLECTIVE HOUSE   145

ACKNOWLEDGMENTS   157

WILD
FAILURE

HALF-PIPE

Friday night, Chevron station bathroom. Boots flat against the poured concrete wall, ass in the sink. I rub a thumb up and down the sweating neck of a bottle of fifty. Asher hid two in the ice freezer out back for us. He let us feel around in the candy bins first, eating until our lips stung in sour pouts.

Hair up or down? I ask. A first-drink question.

Sandy says up. She's still peeing. Strong stream, no hesitation. Twist it. No, not like that. She pulls her miniskirt down, kicks the flusher. Sandy knows how to be a girl.

Sandy grabs my hair, turning it around in her fingers, elastic in her front teeth as she tames it into a top bun. It pinches. I wince, take another long sip.

There, she says. That's perfect.

She pulls a half-empty Diet Coke bottle from her bag, nudges my knees apart. I squeeze it between my thighs. She tips a mickey of Stoli against the open spout. Lip to lip, a smooth pour, not one drop wasted. The sound of the vodka trickle makes me have to pee.

I can't piss in front of you, I say. Go outside.

You're too shy. You're going to get eaten alive if you don't cut that shy shit out. She lights a smoke, leans against the door with her arms crossed.

Just pee.

I'm not going to win this standoff. I pull down my jeans. One hand on the wall to steady a low crouch. It won't come.

Stop looking.

I'm not looking. God, you're conceited.

Okay, then sing a fucking song to distract me.

She sings the national anthem. By true north strong and free a trickle comes, but it runs down my leg. Soaking my sock. I sit down, trying to stop the flow. Sandy laughs.

You're a mess, girl.

I prop an elbow on my right knee and stare at her as I finish peeing. My legs in an open V. Two can play this game. I can feel a soft rush of warm air from the heating vent against my exposed skin. I pretend I don't care. She blows a smoke ring up and ignores me, like she didn't look away first.

I can't believe you sat on that filthy toilet seat.

What, it's just other people's pee on my butt.

We hitchhike to the skate park. I want to walk. It's not that far, but Sandy is impatient, thumbs-out.

A forest-green pickup truck with *Hartley's Sparkling Clean-Up Service* on the side pulls up. I give the driver a once-over, but Sandy just hops in. She tells him we are runaways.

Don't tell me that, he says. I'll have to tell the cops.

No, don't. We're escaping a cult. Morgan here is a child bride. Imagine the bad karma.

He pops the glove compartment, offers us Nutri-Grain cereal bars. I don't like the red ones, my wife keeps buying 'em. Who wants jam with their cereal?

Sandy takes two. I say nothing. While Sandy is distracted, I drink most of the pop bottle. I hold eye contact with the collie sitting behind us, whisper, You're a good dog, yeah, you're a good dog.

She can't hear you, the driver says. It's the first time he's spoken to me. She's deaf, but she sure is loyal.

In the morning, my father pulls the covers off me. Get up. It's twelve-thirty. You're late for work and it's tart bake day. Pearl needs you.

I can't.

Why did you sleep in your clothes? What happened to your jeans?

Both knees are ripped. I cover them as though legs are meant to be private. He gives me a look like he caught me sleeping in a pile of rotting bones. When I open my mouth to respond, my teeth are tiny moths. I'm all mouth.

Sorry, I whisper.

He bought me the jeans last weekend. In secret, because Mom said no jeans should cost more than a week's groceries. He paid on two different credit cards.

After he leaves, I look in the mirror. I'm wearing a shirt I've never seen before. Vans skateboards. The cotton is soft. I look around for the shirt I left the house in. It's nowhere.

I keep getting text messages from TYLER WITH THE COOL HAIR. I don't know who he is, but his texts progress from Hi, you must be hungover! to Your pussy was so tight. I can't stop thinking about you. I type: I think you have the wrong number but don't send it.

When I go to the bathroom to pee, I put my head to my

lap, pucker my mouth around my right knee, scream-cry into the impressive scab.

I put my hands down my pants and feel around for evidence. I know as soon as my finger meets the shoreline. A deep ache. A disconcerting heat.

I scan my brain for a final memory. I see myself trying to ollie on someone's skateboard. Falling. Then my dad waking me up.

By two, I am behind the cash register at my aunt Pearl's pie shop. It's a slow day. I suck on a ginger hard candy, drink cups of cold mint tea. I've showered but I still smell the alcohol on my skin. Thank god Pearl is baking in the back. I crack my knuckles, check myself for bruises. I turn the music up so I don't notice the ringing in my ears.

Later, Pearl finds me kneeling in front of the bulk coffee, pretending to refill the canisters, but really, I'm half sleeping, forehead to a cold bag of medium Ethiopian fair-trade.

She asks: Are you heartsick? Is it a boy?

I guess.

I don't tell Pearl about my life. She says there's something about my face that tells her I'm always in love. She frowns when Sandy appears, because Sandy eats all the free samples.

They're broken cookies, Pearl. Why does it matter if I eat them all? She eats the head of the one shaped like a bunny.

When Pearl tells Sandy that it looks like I'm always in love, Sandy spit-laughs the last cookie.

I don't think Morgan's ever texted a boy back. There's something wrong with her. Speaking of, Tyler says you're ghosting him, but we'll all hang later, right? At the park?

I don't know.

I don't want to admit I don't know who Tyler is in front of

Pearl. Plus, it's rare that Sandy wants to hang out two nights in a row. Maybe she'll call really late and we'll go smoke a joint in the park if she hasn't found anything better to do. I'm a second-tier friend, a backup.

Come on, Tyler's friend Sketch is going to come. It was YOUR idea last night!

It makes more sense then. Sketch is in college. He's the guy all the girls stare at from the top of the half-pipe ramp. Sandy talks about how he once grabbed her ass in a mosh pit then smiled at her. I felt like prey, she said, it paralyzed me.

I've never heard Sketch say a word that has more than one syllable.

When I get home, my uncle is sitting on the back porch. Sometimes he sleeps on our couch when Pearl has long hours on the weekend. He has special needs from the Gulf War, which is how my mother puts it. They tried to send him to Afghanistan, but he had a breakdown before he left. He tries not to drink anymore, but he's off the wagon. When I was little, they told me that and I pictured him literally falling off a wagon.

I join him. He's in sock feet, leaning heavy to the left in a plastic rainbow lawn chair. I thought he might be asleep, but he's got an open beer hiding in a cowboy boot, so he's in fake repose, often leaning toward it. He reaches behind the cedar bush, twists a can loose from a six-pack, and gives it to me. I empty out my water bottle and fill it with beer. We cheers to our little secret party.

I know you're fifteen, so you feel old, but believe me, girl, don't be in any hurry.

It's the first coherent sentence I've heard him say in a while.

Thanks, Uncle Marty.

Because all men are awful.

You're not.

I take a long swig of beer.

Be careful, drinking runs in our family. Up and down both sides.

There's barely a pause before he starts in on 9/11 and why it was perpetuated by the Americans. I tune out. He talks himself into a soft, slow sleep on the lawn chair. I finish all his beer.

My eyes pop open, but all I see is a clear sky, fluttering stars. I'm frightened, until I hear Sandy's voice reaching through the confusing blur, her laugh, then, Look at that bitch getting hers.

Am I falling through the sky? I look down, feel him pushing into me. It hurts so much I have to close my eyes.

I wake again, his face so close to mine, still inside me.

Who are you?

He laughs. What do you mean? This was your idea.

He goes harder, holds my hands down.

Do you like that?

I don't know what to answer, so I turn my head, try to force my eyes to stay open, though they are so heavy, so dry. We are on top of one side of the half-pipe. There's no one else around, except Sandy and Sketch on the other flat side of the ramp. The skateboards lie at the bottom of the half-pipe, swaying in a slow roll. I wonder if the aging wood will crack, or if we'll stay together when we fall.

Sandy's quiet now, because she's giving a blow job. His hands are on her head, but he's looking up at the sky. It's red and pink on the horizon. The park is deserted.

I squeeze my eyes shut, all I hear is their tandem moaning, then the sound of a car peeling down the nearby highway.

This is the best night of my life, Tyler yells, before he comes.

I curl my knees to my chest, a voice inside my head yells at me to sit up, to not go under again. I'm stunned. The night air swirls when I finally get up. He pulls off the condom, a sound like a rubber band snapping. He throws it off the ramp.

Oh man.

I climb down the ladder to the ground, throw up in the grass.

I stay there, digging my shaking fingers into the dirt. He comes up behind me, runs a hand through my hair. Are you okay, baby? You feel cold. Here, have my hoodie.

He covers me in his sweatshirt. It smells like a campfire. We hear Sketch's final moans, then the sound of Sandy laughing.

Will you be my girlfriend? Tyler asks, almost shyly.

I don't tell him this is the only conversation I've ever remembered having with him.

I shrug an okay, and then dry-heave some more.

Sketch knows how to drive. It's 5 A.M.

Why didn't we go home earlier? I ask Sandy. We're going to be in so much trouble.

She hugs me close in the backseat of Sketch's mom's really old compact car. Sandy smells like pineapple perfume and smoke. I guess the car belongs to his mom because a Jewel CD starts playing as soon as he turns the key in the ignition. He pulls it from the player and throws it out the window.

You didn't want to go home, remember? We texted to say we'd be at each other's places.

I check my phone for evidence. I'd sent my dad four lines of heart emojis after I told him I was staying at Sandy's.

Who was this effusive blackout girl?

So where are we going now?

Sandy shrugs. Sketch pulls up in front of a squat apartment building across from the gas station. The guys get out, and I don't move.

I want my bed, I say. Or your house. Let's just go to your house, watch some Netflix.

Coming down with Sandy is always the best part of any night.

You're no fun, she says. This is a big deal. This is his house. He only brings girls he really likes back to his place. Don't fuck this up for me.

⸻

Sketch's apartment smells like garbage. I sit on a ripped ottoman with my arms crossed and stare at the TV. *Planet Earth* is on mute.

Tyler rinses out a coffee mug, fills it with a thick liquor, and hands it to me. It tastes like black licorice. I keep two sips down. The room swirls in and out. I go to the bathroom and pour it down the sink, fill it with tap water. Only the hot water tap works. There is one white towel dangling from a rack, wet and graying, like a detached eyelash. A cake of blue soap with a black vein through the middle, flecks of abandoned beard hairs in the sink.

Sandy sits on Sketch's lap. They kiss a lot. I pull my legs up onto the ottoman. I remember being a kid and pretending the floor was made of lava. Tyler tries to lean into me from the armchair.

You know what would be cool, says Sketch, if you girls kiss on the mouth.

No way, I say.

Sure, Sandy says. I love Morgan. Why wouldn't we kiss?

She walks over to me, a fake-sexy walk, a bumbling baby deer.

Nah, I say. That's stupid.

You homophobic? Tyler asks. 'Cause my brother's a fag.

No. Sandy and I are just friends is all.

Sandy's already straddling me, locking her ankles around my back.

Aw yeah, I hear one of the boys say. In my periphery I see Sketch rubbing the front of his jeans.

I keep my mouth closed, but she pushes my lips open with hers. Our front teeth clank like drawn swords. Her mouth tastes of peppermint and smoke and my stomach lurches. I pull away. I just want to fall asleep against her chest. I want to be watching *Drag Race* in her basement.

I lean back, so Sandy grabs at my tits. Her legs hold me in place. She pushes my breasts around like sand at the beach.

Enough. This is stupid. I stand up so fast that Sandy falls over. I leave without my purse or my phone, run down the long hallway and out the front door.

Sandy yells out the window, You're such a cunt.

I sweet-talk my way onto a late-night bus without fare, tell the driver I got my purse stolen. He says: You should be more careful. You're so young. He drives the bus off the regular route, right down my residential street, stopping in front of my house. I'm so thankful I start to cry. He gives me an avuncular smile.

You shouldn't be drinking so much, young lady.

I get off the bus, stumble a bit up my driveway. As he drives away, even though I love his kind face with everything I have, I give him the finger.

I sneak in the house quietly. In the living room, a glow rises like a bonfire from the television. I try to be quiet, but my uncle pops up, alert.

It's just me, Uncle Marty. It's just Morgan. You're okay.

He stares at me, cranes his neck to peer around me.

No one else?

No one else.

I turn on the bright overhead light to prove it.

He reaches for his bag.

I think I heard someone outside, he says. I'll go do my rounds.

Just go back to bed, Uncle Marty.

No, I've gotta protect you.

He takes a large gun from his overnight bag. As soon as I see the gun, I'm sober.

Uncle Marty, is that loaded?

Of course it's fucking loaded. Otherwise what good is it?

Guns scare me.

He takes that information in. I stay very still, try to speak in a calm, even tone. That's what we're supposed to do when he has episodes.

You stay here, he barks. I mean it, don't move.

He goes out onto the back porch, holds the rifle like he's walking in a military drill. He circles our house, all the sensor lights go on, one by one, like he's in a play and he's stepping into the spotlight for a monologue.

When I guess that he's in front of the house and can't see me through the windows, I run to wake up my mom, who gets up and stands with me in the living room, waiting for him to return. He slides open the patio door.

Everything safe out there? she asks him gently.

He puts the gun back in the bag.

Yup.

I wish you wouldn't do that, Marty. You might scare the neighbors. Some of them get up to jog early in the morning.

I know an enemy from a jogger, he says, like it's preposterous to suggest he'd accidentally shoot someone. She hands him a glass of water. He smells it, then takes a small sip.

She looks at me for a moment, as though just noticing that I'm there.

That's a boy's sweater, she says.

I have a boyfriend now, I say. His name is Tyler.

She looks pleased.

That's good. You're always hanging around Sandy too much. You should meet new people.

Tyler is a shithead's name, says Uncle Marty.

I sleep almost all day Sunday. I reach for my phone and then realize it's not there, that I left it at Sketch's house. I don't even know Sandy's number by heart to try to get it back from her.

I feel briefly untethered, like I may fall away from the ground. My thumbs scroll the air like a dog who runs in place while he's dreaming. I wait it out, the feeling recedes, replaced by a film of calm. My skin has never felt more porous. I pick up the softest sounds.

I ride my bike to the river in a white cotton dress and I wade up to my waist, trying to cool the burning ache.

I don't think about not partying, but I do write myself a note to put in my pocket for next time.

It reads:

Remember not to let anyone inside you, you dumb slut.

I assume Sandy will show up at my house before school on Monday. She doesn't. I am so angry, remembering her hands pawing at me, her cackling laugh, that it does not occur to me that she may be angry at me.

You left me there, alone with them.

I'm eating a green apple in the schoolyard, at our usual spot.

So? You're the one who wanted to be there in the first place. You're the one who wanted to make out with me, like some perv.

She looks hurt. I've never seen Sandy hurt.

You don't do that. You don't leave someone.

She throws my phone at me. It hits me in the chest.

She walks away, toward Sketch's car, waiting for her in the parking lot. I know it will only be a few days until he breaks her heart and I'll get her back.

Forty minutes left of lunch, and without Sandy I just lie down in the grass, reunited with my phone. There are so many texts from TYLER WITH THE COOL HAIR I just delete them all without reading.

I take a series of selfies. Bambi eyes. A filter that peaches my lips.

I scroll back too far and find an unfamiliar video.

The camera moves like the hand that holds it is shaking. Sandy's laugh, the sound of Sketch saying whoa, whoa, a swirl like they don't realize the camera is on.

Then my own face is in the frame, monstrously close. I'm heavy lidded, trying to drink from a bottle of beer, but I keep missing my mouth. Tyler grabs the beer, puts it down and kisses me. We make out like we're eating each other's faces.

Then a few seconds of blackness, and a shot from above: Tyler spreading my legs, my skirt lifted. Sketch's low laugh. Sandy's in the background, like she's standing on the ground under the ramp. Come on, Sketch, leave them alone. Let's go have our own fun.

Wait a sec.

He focuses the close-up on me.

Just do it.

Nah, don't film it.

Come on.

I watch as Tyler's cock goes in me. They both laugh. Tyler

looks into the camera and gives a thumbs-up. The camera moves up to my face. My eyes are closed. My mouth is open.

Sketch, Sandy calls from below, come on.

Sketch whispers, Wake that bitch up.

Tyler shoves me a bit.

Nothing.

He shoves me harder. I blink. My mouth moves into a smile, like I'm dreaming about something really funny.

Yeah, she likes it.

SKETCH. YOU'RE BEING AN ASSHOLE.

Calm the fuck down.

There's a few seconds with the camera still on, as Sketch climbs down to the ground.

You okay, girl? Morgan?

Sketch says: She's fine.

The video stops. The noise of the schoolyard returns. I throw the apple core to the ground. I delete the video.

I skip the rest of the day, pedal up the tallest hill, fly back down. I bike so long my hands go numb, my legs have leopard spots of bike grease. Eventually, I end up on the winding tree-lined road toward Tyler's school.

He's easy to spot, even in the stupid jacket and tie all the private-school kids wear. He takes his tie off his neck really fast when he sees me. Pretends it's a lasso. His blond hair falls, asymmetrical, to cover his right eye. In the daylight his face is more freckle than skin.

I'm surprised, he says, rolling back and forth on his skateboard. You didn't answer one text. You made me feel like a chick.

I press my hands to his chest the way I've seen women do in the movies. I kiss him on the mouth with everything I've got. He's a bad kisser but maybe malleable. When I pull away, he says wow. He holds my hand. I like the way it feels, to be somebody's girlfriend. The private-school girls all look at me and whisper, like I stole their property.

We ride beside each other down the winding hill. I take him to the bench by the river that runs beside the Chevron station. It's heavy tourist season on the boardwalk, lots of khaki shorts and families posing for photographs in front of boats.

I have nothing at all to say to Tyler.

He doesn't notice. He says, I feel like you're the first girl I can really talk to, you know? You're not all caught up in girl stuff.

My emotions are a Magic 8 Ball, like you could shake me and the answer to how are you feeling could change on a dime. I want to ask him what he thinks girl stuff is.

How drunk were you Saturday night? I ask him.

Oh man, pretty drunk. You know.

Do you remember everything?

Of course, babe. I'd never forget it.

I want to ask about the video, but we are interrupted by the sound of someone hollering our names. We look up and see Sandy and Sketch skateboarding toward us.

Sandy pretends we're best friends, hugs me like I'm a child she lost in the park.

She hands me a wine cooler from her backpack.

For a moment it feels good, to have a crew. It feels like enough. I put the bottle to my lips, but the smell makes me gag. I hand it back.

I'm not going to drink today, I say. It's an experiment.

She shrugs, takes a long pull, then sits down next to me.

You punishing me?

For what?

She doesn't answer. Two hours later, every second feels interminable. I discover that sober kissing is boring. The expectation that kissing will be fun when it is not feels almost insulting. Where are my exceptional feelings? Where is the sparkle?

Later, Tyler has my shirt undone, in the backseat of Sketch's car, and I feel nothing. The closest I get to having a feeling is a low-level hum of anger. I'm not certain why. An excuse comes to me. I have homework, I say. Big project.

I jump out of the car. By the time I get home, I've squandered some resolve, some dignity.

I will find new friends.

Then Sandy crawls in through my window in the middle of the night. I am startled to see her dangling headfirst from the window, landing in a collapsing handstand in a pile of my dirty clothes.

My uncle is crazy, I say, sometimes he patrols our house. You shouldn't sneak around out there!

Sandy doesn't respond, just curls up around me.

Take off your dirty boots, I say, but she is fast asleep already. I untie each one, line them up against the wall, stare at the glowing sticker stars on my ceiling.

Late morning. Sandy and I walk into the kitchen. My parents are both at the table. They appear to be sweating, even though it isn't hot.

Hey, Mrs. Stockall, Sandy says, so sweet. It works on every-one. Not my mom.

Sandy, you need to go home. Now.

Later I will learn my mother blames Sandy. She could hear Sandy's voice on the video. That's the one she won't forgive or understand.

It's nothing. It was nothing. It was stupid. I drank a whole bottle. I don't remember anything. No, no, no. Not like that. He says it was my idea anyway. Don't overreact. My god. Just chill. I'm sorry, but it wasn't like I was a virgin or something. Stop acting like this is the end of the world. If you act like this is the end of the world, that's what it becomes.

I am pulled out of school for a week. For my own good. I am not allowed to see Sandy. My father wants to call the police. What kind of name is Sketch anyway? The name of someone who should be in jail.

Don't, please don't. Everyone has a camera now. This just happens. It just happens. It's no one's fault.

My mother rubs my back, says she is sorry it happened, tells me she has made an appointment with a professional.

Later I hear, How can she think it's no one's fault? I hear glass smashing. A hole in the pantry wall the size of her hand. How much more clear can it be?

I just want it to be dropped. It's over. It was a hundred years ago. I say this to Sandy at Shoppers, where I pretend to bump into her.

We try on lip gloss. Cathedral, I read the name on the tube. Her pinky finger dabs my top lip to mark a Cupid's bow.

Yeah. Plus, Sketch is so worried. He went tree-planting up north to avoid it. He's going to write me letters. This is so hard on him.

How did it get out, anyway? It was on my phone. I deleted it.

You saw it?

Yeah.

Sandy puckers, looks at how Ladylike suits her lips in the cheap slice of mirror. It doesn't.

I didn't know that. I didn't even know about it. You weren't mad?

I don't know what I felt. I just wanted it gone.

I saw you kiss him first, you know. You seemed really into him.

Maybe I was.

I don't know why everyone is freaking out about it.

Yeah. Well, it was a shitty thing of Sketch to do, to make a video.

Sandy's face doesn't change as she applies another layer, so I press: It was a totally asshole thing to do in the first place.

Sandy wipes her lips with the back of her hand. Well, we were all pretty drunk. Everybody does stupid stuff when they're drunk. And it was Tyler's girlfriend at the rich-kid school who leaked it. Tyler must have sent the video to himself on your phone before you got it back.

Tyler doesn't have a girlfriend. I'm his girlfriend.

This is the first time I experience a flicker of any feeling for Tyler.

Yeah, I guess he just hadn't broken up with her yet? He said he was going to. Apparently, she's just so dramatic, he didn't want to make a big deal of it. Then she went through his phone, so.

Right.

You have lipstick on your teeth. Here's a trick. She pops her index finger in her mouth like she's sucking it, then pops it out. Won't happen again if you do this every time.

Tyler's texts are relentless and complimentary. I've never loved anyone like you. You're so beautiful. I'm sorry. She's crazy, my ex. So crazy.

I don't respond, but it doesn't dissuade him from sending song lyrics, declarations, endless emojis.

Eventually, he writes: Just say one thing. Just one thing so I know you've read this. I need to know you've forgiven me.

I send him a bull's-eye emoji.

What's that mean!?!

I flash on all the people who may have seen the video, my heavy pebble eyes, face like a slow blur. Somehow that's worse than the porn shots. If only they'd left my face out of it. I could have just been any girl, no girl; detached, meaningless.

I text: Tyler, I think you're boring.

After an initial blurt of question marks, lines of awkward LOLs, eventually he replies: Why can't you forgive me? Let me make it up to you.

I delete the texts.

My mom takes my phone at every opportunity, reading every new text or email, while I stand, arms crossed.

It's for your own good. Someday you'll thank me.

I wear my shortest skirt, my smallest crop top, to school. She doesn't say anything about it anymore. I spend the weekend working at Pearl's and watching documentaries with Uncle Marty. He's not drinking, so he barely speaks.

He spears honeydew chunks and cocktail onions with a toothpick, both swimming in a sweet-and-sour liquid sliding around in the toaster oven tray he eats off of. He's wearing my mom's old bathrobe.

We're watching *Gilmore Girls*. Now, that's the perfect woman, he says suddenly, after two episodes in silence, pausing the screen and pointing to Lorelai Gilmore.

Are you going to tell me what's wrong with you these days, Morgan?

I shake my head.

He shrugs.

It never really helps to do that anyway. People will always tell you it does, but it doesn't. It makes the person listening feel good that they listened.

So what does help?

Marty offers me an onion.

Vigilance.

He un-pauses the show.

Once strangers have seen you naked, it kind of breaks you open, frees something up. Everyone else is having nightmares about walking into class with no clothes. That's already happened to me. I can move on to worrying about getting into college or my inevitable death.

Whenever a girl gives me side-eye, I think about saying: You have a pussy. So do I. Get over it.

No one says anything about Tyler's cock, his high five with Sketch, slits for eyes, exuberant grin.

TYLER WITH THE COOL HAIR sends seventeen texts, all mostly invitations to come out: I'm at the half-pipe and I'm so sad here without you.

Finally I write: I don't want to go out. I don't want to see you.

But I love you, he writes, I have to see you.

I don't answer while Uncle Marty and I make our way through several more episodes, wordless, finishing every pickle in the fridge. My tongue is cold and hurts by the time I fall asleep.

I wake with a start to the vibration from my phone.

TYLER WITH THE COOL HAIR: I'm outside your window. Come out.

Go home, I text, snuggle back under the flannel couch throw. When the motion lights flicker outside, I note the sliding patio door askew, the absence of a deep snore from Marty on the adjacent couch.

I'm up, running, trying to stop what I know could happen, and it sounds like a crack of lightning in the sky when it does.

WILD FAILURE

They're driving their failing relationship into the desert. Jasper pulls the car onto the edge of the thinning highway and gets out to take photos. Teprine presses a palm against the rental car window, comparing her skin to the burning hues beyond. She props her phone up, clicks a lazy burst of landscape shots. She will love the memory of having been here.

She doesn't understand how to travel. All she sees is endless metaphor. Humans are small, the earth is infinite and murderous. If I get out of the car, I will fall off the planet. The seatbelt cleaves her chest. She appreciates the way it holds her down. Her skin isn't enough. Contained, she sucks on a mango Popsicle from the last gas station, her fingers smell like hand sanitizer, applied hourly.

There's a tenderness to the desert's red landscape. She's never seen a desert before.

Teprine turns forty this month. She re-met Jasper nearly a year ago, at the supermarket the day after she turned thirty-nine. They knew each other from around the community, that queer small town nestled tight in the mouth of every sprawling city. She was wearing sweatpants with a coleslaw stain splattered across both knees. It looked like cum and she didn't care. All the same, she'd tried to hide when she looked up from the Concord grapes and saw him smelling a tomato. She counted out four minutes in the bakery but ended up behind him in the checkout line anyhow.

"Hey, how's it going?" She hadn't spoken out loud in two days and could barely manage this strained greeting.

"I'm getting divorced," he said.

She'd blushed, embarrassed. "Me too."

He was remarkably handsome, even under the anemic lights of Fiesta Farms. She'd never have asked him out, but the divorce had made her emotionally reckless. Also, she was more afraid of the open sky than social rejection.

Holding her green plastic grocery bags, she was a recovered agoraphobic in danger of a relapse, clinging to the anchor of walls, familiar bus routes, the comfort of crowds. He felt most at peace while hiking off into the distance, free from human scrutiny. But they didn't yet know these secrets about each other.

After two shy dates, they kissed in a way that anesthetized the former heartbreak. Alone, they were floating heads. Together, they reminded each other that a body is capable of heedless elation.

Teprine can keep things in perspective. The car is a mobile piece of the familiar. The familiar is a mental salve. Whenever the car stops, her heart runs up into her throat. Her thoughts blur and blend. She was raised in a valley, her bedroom window opened to sprawling meadows. She felt safe in the warm, tight farmhouse, anchored by packed snow.

She licks the Popsicle stick clean. The thrum of her spatial anxiety sounds like an amplifier on its last legs. When the outside gets too overwhelming, she pictures curling up under the drive shaft like a cat. She touches the window, the only barrier between her vacated body and the edge of Joshua Tree National Park. She can see that it is beautiful. Of course. But it's like looking at a pastoral oil painting she doesn't feel anything for. The view could have been a greasy portrait in a hotel room. She can see Jasper in the rearview mirror taking endless photos. They haven't passed another vehicle in almost an hour.

He gets back in the car. She bites the Popsicle stick. The rush of air conditioning tucks her hair behind her ears. Soothing. She makes her face into an expression that approximates relaxed and easygoing. I'm a fun girl!

Jasper smiles at her and squeezes her leg. He pulls out a map, runs his finger along a line so thin it looks like an accidental pencil scrawl. "This old road is supposed to be amazing," he says. "Should we take it?"

He is so excited to veer off course, she doesn't want to say no, but immediately imagines the car breaking down, and no one finding their bodies for days. They have one small bottle of coconut water in a tote bag in the backseat, one cold brew coffee between her thighs. She hears herself say, "Let's take the regular highway, it's going to get dark."

He pulls away, a half frown.

She knows he's disappointed. Nothing makes him feel more alive than when he's timeless, rudderless, alone in the open wild. Later, in the hotel, Teprine will lie awake as he snores gently and feel a shame so acute that she will long to be stranded on a dirt road waiting for the sun to kill them.

In a few days, Teprine will nearly die, but she doesn't know that now. Worrying about it for almost forty years hasn't prepared her.

They'd been planning the trip for months. She took out books from the library about women who traveled to far-flung places by themselves. They talked about being transformed. She wanted that. She was sick of her face in the grim mirrors at the gym. She talked to her therapist about calming self-talk. She wrote a hierarchy of fear on the back of a red paper takeout menu at the café near her apartment. She bought a leather passport holder, and decided which dress was luckiest to fly in. She chose a brown cotton knee-length, with sky-blue birds embroidered on the hem. She stashed travel-sized tubes of Tylenol, ginger candies, and hand sanitizer into the front pocket of her backpack.

As you drive out west in America, the world opens up, the same way it does in Canada. The sky grows bigger until Teprine feels like a spider in a bathtub. She is not transformed. She can't write an inspiring memoir about overcoming the adversity of her agoraphobic tendencies. The disappointment feels worse than she imagined it ever could.

Teprine has two patchy bruises on her inner elbow from a blood test. She didn't want to get sick in America, so she got every test. If she were rich, she'd request a full-body PET scan every few years. The nurse said your veins are impossible. She doesn't like to contemplate the existence of veins. Basic biology in grade nine made her gag. She can barely register that she lives inside a body. She and Jasper have this in common. But, having found each other in the haze of post-divorce sadness, their bodies become the whole point. On this trip, as at home, when they're not otherwise occupied, they are having sex. When she hears him unbuckling his belt, her mouth opens on its own, her back arches. Even if he's just changing quickly into swim clothes, the metal clink makes her body ready.

She doesn't like to lie on her back—at the doctor's office, in yoga class, during meditation—it makes her feel as though she could float away. But she longs to be underneath him, anchored. In 29 Palms Inn, a pink adobe cottage, he held the bed frame above her head uselessly to keep it from banging against the wall, but the sound was unstoppable. She used to move all around the room when she fucked someone. Now she just wanted to be still, his full weight on top of her.

On their first morning of the trip, before they were really awake, they were fucking fast and frenzied, as though battling through disconnection. Teprine couldn't turn her brain off, it processed the many layers of what was occurring, even while her mouth was saying all the things he likes to hear, even while her body was responding.

They have tried to break up, but they can't stop having sex.

She wants to be someone for whom sanity is not something to be labored for, the kind of person who can be present in every moment, who can walk into the desert with some water and a map and a sense of adventure, whose only concern is an excellent photograph. Faced with the unfamiliar, she's in full histamine flutter.

But in a hotel bed, the new and the familiar collide. Jasper has all the control in this game, she feigns helplessness. She never tires of his commanding voice, his soft, theatrical coercion, his hand over her mouth.

There's a freedom in the constraint.

Two hours before their departing flight, Jasper had thrown a hitch in the plan.

"I love you," he said. "But something is missing."

There wasn't a word for it, but it was missing. He rubbed his chest in a circular motion.

"Be more specific," Teprine said, though she didn't need him to be. Everyone knows when they're being broken up with, however kind and vague the rejection, even if it happens right after he makes you come thirteen times in a row in the back of his Mazda5 in the Park 'N Fly lot outside the airport.

"I love you," he repeated, as if that made it significant.

She furrowed her brow. Then, smoothing down her skirt, she lifted the wrapper from a child's granola bar off her thigh like a Band-Aid. She had non-returnable tickets. She had a goal of walking into the desert and staying alive.

"I still want you to come on this trip," he said.

She knew, if she were a strong and independent woman, or the narrator in an anthemic R&B song, she would simply strut out of that Mississauga parking lot and into her own good enough life. But she didn't cancel the trip.

"I guess it'll be like our farewell tour," she said. She was angry, but compared with her fear, rage was more of an irritant than a serious problem.

At departures, he did his weekly shot of testosterone in the bathroom before they went through security. He was too flustered before they left to do it at home and didn't want to have to explain what it was to likely transphobic security agents at customs. He claimed to not notice any differences, but every time he did it, his grip on her wrists tightened.

It goes without saying, Teprine is not a good flier. Agoraphobics never are. Thankfully, Ativan engenders a feeling of being absent from the cruelties of the self. After dissolving one milligram under her tongue, Teprine was able to board the plane to Arizona.

She had a moment of clarity while sitting beside Jasper in the O'Hare departure lounge on a stopover: this would be their last trip together. It was almost a neutral thought. A fact. Sometimes she gets a glimpse of her real personality while taking anti-anxiety medication. Perhaps underneath the screaming blur of irrational fear, she's actually pretty chill.

They didn't even get a chance to unpack their bags in the hotel room before his breath on her neck became urgent, and he whispered, "You're mine," and those words buoyed her against every known uncertainty.

———

Teprine will turn forty on the day they arrive in Los Angeles near the end of their trip. Forty felt like a relief to Jasper. Everyone who already has kids says turning forty is a relief. But Teprine finds little solace in the tins of cream meant for the infinitesimal area under each eye. She wishes time could pause. When she sees babies, she sometimes involuntarily cries out with longing, and has to pretend it's just a coughing fit.

A week before the trip, Jasper's four-year-old looked at Teprine while she was reading him a bedtime story and with weird toddler solemnity said, "When the end of the world comes, I'm going to dig a hole for my family. And you can come too." After he said that, Teprine laughed and then went to the bathroom to cry because she knew she probably wasn't going to be around for another birthday, let alone the apocalypse, in this kid's life.

Jasper appears, to Teprine, both scared of their relationship and scared of not being in their relationship. As soon as the breakup is final, he reaches for her all day long. She's not sure how she should react, so she lets her body make the decision.

They stop along Route 62 at a series of giant dinosaur sculptures. She takes photos of him pretending to be eaten by the *Tyrannosaurus rex*. He texts the pictures to his kids. She looks around at the small grouping of desert houses and wonders if she should just stop the trip and rent an apartment. She could be one of the girls in flimsy dresses selling pies at the bakery along the highway. She could rename herself something simple like Jen. Jen drinks her iced hibiscus tea behind the counter at the bulk spice store. She could settle down. Jen could be easygoing.

Later that night, Jasper calls the kids. They critique the photos he sent. They're not real dinosaurs, they say. You don't look scared enough.

The first twenty steps are always the most difficult. It's when an agoraphobic will most likely turn around. Teprine left the guest house in Tucson on their second day of the trip, heading toward a bus stop two blocks away. Even as the ground began to tilt, and she gripped the edges of her white sundress, she kept going. She got to the bench beside the bus stop. Exposure therapy only works if you keep going, travel up and down the arc of panic.

Her skirt rose up, and she could see the beautiful bruises on her thighs. Jasper doesn't like them. I don't want to hurt you, ever. I love you. But she likes to see her resilience reflected back. The bus stop was across from a deserted schoolyard. The only people around were inside their cars. She tried to read an essay by Susan Sontag, but she could only read one line: *Whenever people feel safe, they will feel indifferent.*

What does it mean to accept your limitations?

The bus arrives. She sits near the front. She looks out the bus window. She would feel better if she went back to the guest house. Sometimes she feels jealous of people who stay home, who frame their mental health issues as disability issues that should be accommodated in a just society. But she feels that if you stay home, the agoraphobia wins.

A man got on the bus and stared at her tits for so long without stopping that she almost admired his singular focus. She clenched and unclenched all the muscles in her legs while counting and trying to breathe slowly, trying to turn so the man couldn't see her. As she shifted, so did his gaze. She got off the bus quickly so the man wouldn't follow.

At Sparkroot Café the baristas were femmes in vintage sundresses, tattooed arms, much like her dress, her arms. One of them ran a finger along the deer tattoo on Teprine's bicep and complimented it. Teprine sat at a table and took her journal out of her tote bag. The Bon Iver album that played, the Blue Bottle coffee, all of it combined to mollify her against the unknown. She knew all those tastes, the sound of those chord progressions. *Tomorrow I will be more adventurous,* she wrote in the journal. *Today I will get settled.* But she knew that she'd come back to this café the next day, and sit at this table, and order the same thing.

Teprine tried to join Jasper at an academic talk on poetic embodiments at the university. The map didn't betray the length of city blocks. No one else was walking. She flagged a cab, and the driver said, In another month, you wouldn't be able to just stand there, flagging me down. You'd be dead. That's how hot it gets here. You should be more careful.

She got a small jolt of pleasure that she'd taken a risk, even a dumb accidental one.

Fifteen years earlier, Teprine was so afraid to take the subway that she would slip a token into the slot, get halfway down the stairs to the platform, and then turn around and run back up until she reached the safety of the sidewalk. She would spend days in her apartment, leaving only when she absolutely had to. She felt doomed to a life of very little, a small-scale world. She went to a doctor at the university walk-in clinic, and after a two-minute assessment was told that people with her condition either kill themselves or go on medication. She got a vial of yellow-and-white pills that made her mouth dry. Teprine has been off SSRIs for a decade. But sometimes the feeling comes back, like a virus, seeping in when things get overwhelming, or whenever she's somewhere new.

Teprine thinks the *B* in *LGBT* is the most embarrassing letter in the acronym. Her ex-girlfriend, a butch, used to get upset about Teprine potentially leaving her for a trans guy. When she started dating Jasper, her ex returned some books to her house and said, "I knew it. I knew you wanted to date a trans guy." She thinks about dating another femme, the way the younger queers do, with their #femmeforfemme name-plate necklaces, but feels too old. Sex would always feel like play-acting, looking over her shoulder for the camera. It's possible there is no one she could date who wouldn't feel un-easy about her bisexuality.

A study comes out that says bi women have terrible mental health. Teprine only reads the headline.

Though naturally disinclined toward activities that involve either, Teprine attends a group hike. It is led by a blond yoga enthusiast called Leslie. She wants Jasper and Teprine to stand with the saguaro cactus, as some sort of ritual. Teprine follows along, despite feeling like too much of an East Coast cynic to appreciate it. The hike was suggested by Jasper's scholar friends, who are interesting and awkward. They wear expensive clothes, but something is always untucked or aloft. Glasses don't stay on their faces.

"I'm afraid of heights," she tells Leslie, because it is easier to say that than to explain that she is afraid of space and air. "I may be slow or leave early," she continues. Leslie offers her a warm smile. Sometimes just admitting her anxieties allows them to retreat.

"To allow the cactus to communicate," Leslie says, "stay still."

They watch her being still, and slowly stop fidgeting and

stretching to imitate her pose. When Teprine tries to stand still, she feels as though she remains in motion.

"Try to listen to what the saguaros are saying," Leslie says.

No one else finds this instruction peculiar, and Teprine begins the ascent. If she stays far from the edge, she will feel grounded, so she hugs the hill. She imitates normal human walking, takes photos of the cactus, the view. She watches the faces of others express wonderment at their surroundings. She tries to make her face look like their faces.

She walks a little farther up the hill before she feels it start. The panic comes initially as an impulse to sit on the ground, even though she's wearing a short dress and everything in the desert looks as though it would prickle or itch. She wants to get close to the earth even though it would render her a spectacle or cause concern. But she doesn't sit. She keeps walking, every step farther from her body as it moves.

Teprine speeds up, walking faster than the group, as though trying to outrun her fear. She is thrilled to see a bench on the side of the mountain. A sign beside it asks that visitors sit and offer prayers. There is a makeshift altar beside the bench where people have left objects—brightly colored dolls, photos of people who have died. There's a faded photocopy of a picture of the singer Mia Zapata affixed to the altar. She remembers how shocked she was to hear about Zapata's murder. Teprine liked to listen to her music while walking home from work after last call. She practiced her fight face while listening to Zapata's screaming vocals.

Teprine was occasionally followed home from work. One

night she dropped a sweater as she ran from a pursuer, slamming her apartment door in the drunk man's face. He'd scratched at the door with his nails, a sad feral cat. In the morning she found him curled up on her doorstep, wrapped in her bright pink cardigan, sucking on the wool.

A snake zips under the bench. She pulls her legs up. She practices breathing slowly and intentionally, then stands up and continues up the trail.

She's completely lost track of the group, if they are ahead or behind her. She stands still, trying to hear footsteps or chatter, camera shutters clicking. She only hears her own pulse in her ears. The saguaros don't say anything.

Make yourself seem bigger, the guidebook said, if you ever see a mountain lion. Teprine read it out loud to Jasper in the car. Maintain eye contact.

"Don't worry, babe," he'd said, "we won't see a mountain lion." He spoke with a certainty she envied.

The cougar is curled up, sleeping, comma shaped, a breathing rock, when she rounds a curve in the trail. Distracted by the possibility of every kind of peril, Teprine didn't take notice of real danger until it was ten feet away. A sudden intake of breath, a retreat. *This would be funny to everyone I know. That I'm going to die this way. Ironic.*

She could lie down and just offer herself. The worrying would be over. She stands so still. And there isn't even a noise to startle him. Perhaps just the smell of her, the way she must always smell like fear, wakes him up.

She yells, lifts her arms. She is five feet tall. She tries to mimic a saguaro. Ordinary. She belongs here. Eye contact. It doesn't work. It isn't working. He walks toward her. She remembers that her eyes are shielded in oversized shades, and she pulls them off, throws them into the wind. She stares him down. She has never stared so hard. She hears herself yell again and the yells echo. He retreats, at first like a slow-moving liquid and then, hearing the oncoming group of hikers behind her, at a furious clip. She watches him go. It looks like he's flying up the hill.

When Teprine was younger and first suffering and didn't know why, she would do anything not to be alone, though the labor involved in being around people exhausted her. She would choose men and women she had nothing to say to, lying in their beds so that she wouldn't die alone in hers. She'd rather hold a cock in her hand for a few minutes than face certain suicide if she went home by herself. She thought about suicide not as an act she would participate in, but as something that would happen to her. So she'd walk to the bar and order two drinks, just to make sure she had a witness. She needed a witness so that she could keep her body together.

"You are so lucky to be alive," says Leslie. She gathers Teprine in her arms. Her hair smells like carrot greens. "That could have been it. That could have been all there was to your life," she babbles.

That night Jasper whispers, "I'm so grateful for you, I'm so grateful for you," into her mouth, parting her legs with his knee.

In LA, they drive to Malibu, stretch towels along the sand, and celebrate Teprine's birthday. At the beach it's as though they have crawled inside every film, every TV show, and they are imaginary. They rent a guest house in the backyard of a wealthy couple in the Palisades. At night, she becomes beautiful stillness, falling back into the sheets.

Jasper places one hand on her mouth, whispers, "You're mine forever. Forever."

She knows *forever* means one more day, one flight home. He exhales in a groan, all the beauty in that cool room.

MORE HOLY

When I'm twelve, I have a pet lamb named Wilbur. I feed her powdered milk mixed with water that I funnel into an old beer bottle. She pulls on the rubber nipple, enthralled with me. The green-and-white Labatt 50 label sparkles my palm. The other sheep run from me, but Wilbur thinks I'm her family. She isn't scared of the dog. Sometimes I let her come inside the house, then pour molasses into the dog food bowl. When I'm an adult and I meet children who are twelve, I often say, Twelve is the best age!

My parents taught me to say *I'm fine* when anyone asked *How are you?* It doesn't sound right when I say it, but I don't know what else to say. I don't want to bother anyone with my real feelings. My family listens to public radio, plays comedy records, sings folk songs while doing the morning and nightly chores. When I meet people who express sorrow or anger, and explain what they need but don't get—these are people I want to be around, as though I can wordlessly learn to feel and express feelings by being around their leaking faces, their longing. When adults ask me what I want to be when I grow up, I say an actor. Imagine spending your life pretending to feel everything so deeply. I rent *Fame* so many times from the rack of VHS tapes at the corner store that Mrs. Johnston tells me to keep it.

As a child I spend a lot of afternoons lying on the forest floor, a bed of wet cedar, an audience of softwood branches.

Wilbur is the only one who isn't afraid of the coyote.

I grow up to make films.

Going on tour to promote an independent film sounds glamorous, but when you're thirty-eight and rethinking all your life choices, it just means you're taking panicked naps in dozens of near-identical hotel rooms. On the last night of touring, I think I see Simon sit down in the front row. I'm not sure it's him. The lights are too bright. I'm standing onstage wearing the same pale blue dress with the vine-leaf print at the hem that I'd worn for twelve other events. I'm introducing the film, saying the same few sentences I always say, and then I walk up the aisle to pace in the lobby until it's time to come back again for a Q&A. I'm proud of this film, but I am tired of it. When I watch it, I can only see how it might have been improved. I want to start something new, but I spend most of my time thinking about me and Jamie. How our relationship could last. I have artistic pursuits, but ever since I met Jamie, my one quasi-intellectual pursuit is how one sustains a turbulent love. I turn to poetry. I watch a lot of porn.

Jamie is usually with me at events, but tonight they stayed back at the hotel, working on a deadline. Jamie is a journalist. We spend a lot of time looking up at each other from the glowing lip of our laptops. Right before the screening, I'm trying to get dressed, and they want me again. I just need them to do up my dress. They try to take it off instead. It rips a little. Sorry, they whisper. When I say a firm no, not a playful no that would lead to some kind of fantasy sequence, they flop back on the bed and pop their hand in their pants. A sulking face. I grab my purse and leave, doing my dress up in the elevator.

I've been queer for twenty years. It took me a long time to figure out my weakness is for hard-won masculinity. Especially any kind that has an edge of softness. Jamie looks like they'd fight a bear for me. They often want me, in a physical way, but I want them in an emotional way that is unyielding. Sometimes when they're fucking me, I think that I could probably be anyone and in that moment they wouldn't care. They'll always be the one who is more beloved. I know they will one day leave me. I think that keeps me from getting bored. I have only ever loved someone with that kind of intensity once before. And he's in the front row of the theater, looking twenty years older. Simon.

At the Q&A, I get a lot of questions that the asker thinks are unique but I've fielded dozens of times. There's always one asshole who asks about feminist hysteria. I have quips, snaps, and diversions at the ready. This is the last event. I walk up the waxy wooden stairs and the moderator hands me the microphone. And that's when I see Simon for real, with the house lights up. He's bald now. I can't feel my feet.

In 1988, Simon is singing "Jesus Is the Rock" when he grabs my hand. Our pew is crowded with youth group kids, so the sides of our legs are touching all the way down. There is so much happening in my body that being still is impossible. I am almost thirteen. Simon is seventeen. When he leans down to say, Peace be with you, as the minister instructs us to do, I feel his stubble across my cheek. I have never felt more holy.

"He's had a rough life," my mother tells me in the car on the way to the grocery store. I sit in the backseat with a sheaf of paper in my lap, writing to Simon. My stationery has peaches and butterflies along the border. When you press your nose against the matching envelopes, you can smell pie. I see Simon every few months at the county youth group gatherings. He lives an hour away. That my mom thinks she can tell me anything I don't already know about Simon is crazy. Of course he's had a hard life. A hard life is an interesting life. Unlike mine.

I pretend to be tough in my letters to Simon. I write very basic things about being twelve and three-quarters and living on a farm. I write in green cursive. I don't tell him how much I like to read, or how much I appreciate the town librarian. Our library is in the basement of a church, and there is a corner of it reserved for English books. I've read almost all of them. This week, the only book left is a biography of Elvis.

When the new Scholastic Book Club flyer comes out, it's the best day of the season. I don't write to Simon about that either.

———

Simon's letters to me are scrawled in barely decipherable masculine lettering, my name and address on plain white envelopes. They hold so many feelings—about his parents, about the factory where he's started to work after quitting school, about his friend who had dropped acid and then killed himself. I read them so much they are memorized by the time a new one arrives. I love how he ends the letters. He tells me how much he loves me, how special I am, how beautiful. Beautiful? I'm still growing out a bowl cut, little straggles of dirty-blond hair. My most prized possession is a white lace trainer bra from the Sears catalog. I even wear it to bed, hoping it will help spur growth.

———

Even though I know what it feels like to grip bailer twine inside my fists, I know my hands are going to be soft throughout my life. I'm going to be among books. I'll go to university and I'll have options. Kids around here have no options, I hear adults say around the snack table after Sunday school. My brother is starting grade eight. The neighbor comes over to fix the tractor. He looks at my brother and says, "Eighth grade, just about quittin' time, eh?" My brother wears thick glasses. His favorite hobby is math.

———

When I'm a kid, I think we are poor because there is a hole under the gas pedal of the van we use to haul the sheep, and tufts of pink insulation peeking out from my bedroom wall. I fall asleep to the soft scratching of the mice who live under my bed. But there is something different about us. My mom says "We can't afford that" about twenty times a day, and the girls at school make fun of my clothes, often my brother's hand-me-downs. But there is a difference between me and most of the kids I know. It's something to do with the way my friends grimace when my mom makes carob brownies. I practice dancing like the girls in the Whitesnake videos, but it does not come naturally. My best friend's parents are in their thirties but don't have their own teeth. Her mom is one of fourteen children, her grandmother got married at thirteen. My mom says it's because the Catholic Church hates women.

I overhear my best friend's mom calling my mom uppity. They say "She's been to college" like it's an insult.

My mom says, "We're broke, but we're not poor."

Sometimes, when Simon is upset about a girl, he calls me. I curl the phone cord around my wrist, pulling it as far away from the base in the living room as I can, and lean against the near-closed bathroom door. He often cries. I say, "Simon, I love you." There is usually a long pause, and then he says, "You're the only one who really does."

"You know Simon is a man," my mother says. "He dates women his own age." We are driving through the flattened hay of a makeshift parking lot at the county fair.

"His girlfriend's name is Tammy," I say, proving to her that I know some things too.

A few months later, his letters stop coming.

"I hear Simon went off to the army," my mom says at dinner. "I saw his mom at the mall. He's going to Kosovo soon."

When I am sixteen, Simon visits me on the farm. He has been overseas for several years. Now that I'm older, he could have expectations. It settles in my chest like a mildly pleasant pressure. Years later I will understand that Simon's appeal was largely his unavailability. There was no possibility of queerness, so I settled for distance and fantasy and never having to deal with a real boy. Real boys, in my class, were mostly unappealing. Unless one had a crush on me, which gave me something to talk to other girls about.

At the time of Simon's visit, I have a boyfriend I feel ambivalent about. I haven't felt a real attraction to anyone since

Simon, mostly because I don't yet understand that the operatic feelings of loyalty I have toward my best friend mean something. I'm hungover because in order to have sex with my boyfriend I have to drink an entire bottle of wine. When Simon tells me on the phone that he got married, I feel a strange mix of jealousy and relief.

He shows up on a Saturday afternoon. When we hug, it feels as if I am made of carbonation. There is something between us, and that something makes it very clear that there is nothing between my boyfriend and me.

I show Simon my tattoo of a peace symbol. I tell him about how I don't think we should kill people in the Middle East for oil and corporate interests. The Gulf War is raging. He says, "I figured you and I might disagree about that. It's hard being over there. I saw a lot of things I can't unsee."

As he drives down the two-lane highway that leads to town, I can tell that Simon is sad in a way I've never seen anyone sad before. He drives too fast. I don't know what to say as he swerves across the white highway line and back to our side. He doesn't apologize. He doesn't seem to notice. I grip my seatbelt.

"I missed you," I say, and when I say it, I realize I'm testing him. He smiles, but lays heavy on the gas.

"I missed you too, kid. Thinking about you has gotten me through a lot of hard times."

I am pleased to hear this. I have made an impression; someone thinks of me when I am not there. Simon guns it again. A semitruck is approaching us, we are too close to the middle line. The truck blares its horn, and Simon moves at the last moment.

My voice is higher than I want it to be when I ask, "Are you okay?"

"Don't worry, baby, don't worry," he says to the windshield. "I only go as fast as makes sense."

We fly by the trailer where Cathy lives. Her mom is in the yard hanging flowered bedsheets, and normally I'd wave to her, but we're going so fast she's a blur. I think about how many miles we are from town, from having to stop at a light. The town has only two lights. I wonder if I should jump out at one.

Simon is worried his marriage is ending. He's fucked up now. I want out of the truck. But I keep smiling, flirting, even though he is scaring me. I stick my chest out, I curl one string of hair around my finger.

"Why don't we stop the truck?" I ask.

He doesn't answer.

"I'm going to throw up."

He finally hears me and pulls the truck up to a lookout area. We stop so fast my seatbelt feels like a knife. No one ever uses this place except teenagers at night. Simon takes a deep breath. His hands are still gripping the wheel. I go to open the door, but it's auto-locked.

"Let's get out?" I say in a sunny way, as if the drive has been completely normal.

"Sorry," he whispers.

But he doesn't open the door. Instead, he turns on the radio. It's a heavy metal ballad from about five years ago. We danced to it at a youth group party.

"I like this one. It reminds me of you."

"Me too," I say, hiding one hand behind me, pulling on the door handle so hard I fear I might break it off.

"Your boyfriend, he treats you well? I hope your boyfriend treats you well. You deserve the best."

I don't know what to say to that. I don't treat my boyfriend well. I find him boring, but I can't do anything about it. There are only six boys in my grade ten class and I'm related to three of them. I had to date someone, so I chose a classmate's older brother. Simon is only a year older than my boyfriend. When I look at Simon, I feel older than him, though he is now married, and he has, presumably, killed people.

"I need to go outside," I say. "I'm going to be sick."

"Oh," he says, as though just waking up. He clicks the lock and I stumble out. I run toward a bush and hide behind it. Once I'm there, I don't need to throw up anymore. But I lean over as if I do.

It's too cold to walk anywhere from here. I could follow the riverbank into town, but it gets rocky. And it would be melodramatic. I look back. He is leaning against the front of the truck and has lit a cigarette. He looks normal again. I remember reading vespers together at night at youth camp. He opens a pack of Export A's and offers me one as I approach the truck. I make a show of wiping my mouth as though I'd just thrown up.

I shake my head.

"You must really be hungover," he says.

I want to say, I'm carsick from you driving like a maniac, but I don't. I need to keep everything calm. I lean against the front of the truck too. The song is ending inside.

"You're so lucky to be young. You haven't made mistakes yet."

He puts his hands on my hips, a thumb through a belt loop of my burgundy corduroys. I lean my face against his chest, the way I used to. Even though I'd just contemplated hypothermia to get away from him, my body responds the way it always has. He holds me closer, our bodies pushed together completely. When I stand this way with my boyfriend, he gets hard right away, but I don't feel that from Simon.

I've learned to pause in moments of extreme feeling to see if it's a real feeling. It usually isn't. But this is.

On the way home, he drives slower. He puts one hand on my leg as he drives, lightly moving a few fingers up and down just above my knee. I want to ask, Are we soulmates? I have flashes of the night before, in my friend's basement, my boyfriend taking me from behind up against a chest freezer. Even after the wine, it was awkward from start to finish. What Simon is doing, just touching my leg, makes me want to take my clothes off. I look out the passenger seat window, at the trees flickering like an old film reel. I catch glimpses of a deer, a rusted-out car, a coyote.

I want him to move his hand up farther, but he doesn't. I start to feel as though I have never wanted anything more. I pretend to adjust in my seat, so his hand ends up a little higher on my thigh. I press my lips against my fist. I can't control the way I'm breathing or understand if it's loud enough for him to hear above the roar of his pickup truck on the gravel. He taps his fingers to the music, moving higher up. We hit a bump and his hand moves up by accident, knuckles me soft in a place, but it's only there for maybe two seconds before he puts both hands back on the wheel to turn into our driveway. In that second, I am coming in waves, squeezing my legs together, completely undone. I have never had an orgasm before.

We both look ahead for the last few hundred yards up to the house. I don't know if he knows. I am stunned, running my shaking hands through my hair. When he stops the truck, we see my mother raking up leaves in the front yard. The neighbor has dropped off their four-year-old, who I look after every Saturday night. He is jumping in the leaves. I want to kiss Simon, but we hug instead. He looks almost impatient for me to get out of the truck, so I do.

I feel a tenderness for my mother that I don't express as we both watch Simon drive away.

"How was the visit?"

"Fine."

Two years later, I will come out at college because a girl with a buzz cut will kiss me at a ladies' night, mouths sticky with kamikaze shooters. I'll remember that feeling from the pickup truck and all the pieces will fit together. When she breaks up

with me, I will be so distraught that I'll drink nearly a whole
bottle of tequila and kneel down in the middle of a busy street
while it pours rain, daring cars to hit me.

Instead of walking down the stage steps the way I usually do,
I exit through the side door, into the green room with its
room-temperature bottles of water and abandoned Styrofoam
cups. Later my publicist hands me a note from Simon. *Congratulations! You've come so far!* His phone number. That same
masculine scrawl. I slip it into my wallet. I don't call.

When I get back to the hotel, Jamie has not written one word
in my absence. I don't tell them about Simon. They are curled
over a "Stepbrother Wakes Me Up!" video. We act it out for
hours. At some point they say, "I think we should get married." I can't tell if they are using their fantasy story voice or
their real voice.

As dawn flickers through the hotel window that will never
open, Jamie tells me a story about hitchhiking on boats when
they were young. When I talk to them, I have no choice but
to use my real voice. I give them all of me, every vulnerable,
shaky word. When Jamie talks, it's as though I've never listened closely to anyone else before. Everything they say is
gold. Have you ever been talking to someone and thought,
Oh, this is my real voice! These are my true thoughts! It's rare

for me to feel that way. But when I do, it endears me to whom-
ever I'm speaking with. I want to ask Jamie: *Do you also feel*
unguarded and absolutely yourself right now? In the majority of
my conversations I am bending around. I speak the way they
speak. I change my words. I change my tone, trying to be understood, avoid conflict, and make them like me.

Jamie pauses the story. They look as though they might fall
asleep. And then they say, "I think I need to be alone. I love
you, but not in the right way." They put their head between
my legs and ask if they can sleep there. "I adore you, I adore
you," they say as they fall asleep.

We go to a dear friend's wedding, and I cry through the ceremony. When we get in the car, Jamie says it's definitely over.
They're looking at me the way someone looks after they come
and sex becomes indecipherable. I'm the movie that keeps
playing and as you fall asleep, you notice the porn actors look
tired or restless, when minutes earlier they were everything
you ever wanted to look at. All that fake, holy screaming.

No adult can abandon another adult, says the codependent
reader in the bookstore where I walk the next day. I take a
photo of the page because I am struck by this sentence. I feel
abandoned by Jamie, but maybe it is not possible. You're allowed to change your mind about anyone. There are so few
people I get attached to that, when I do, it feels like they're
murdering me if they leave.

OH, EL

Jim and Eleanor stood in the middle of a frozen pond. It was early March, around midnight, and the trip had been Jim's idea. He felt liberated from the city an hour south, and like a superhero for walking where he normally swam.

Eleanor, the only other human for miles, felt one second away from breaking through the ice. Imagined the hypothermia, certain death underneath fourteen visible stars. The pond was a bull's-eye in a circle of trees, thick and unforgiving. Eleanor didn't trust rural areas. There was a break between the trees for a small path to Jim's car, a 1991 four-door Toyota hatchback. Grass green.

He held his arms akimbo and breathed in deep under the glow of the almost-full moon. He said something predictable, like, "Isn't this moment magical, El? I'm so glad I could share this place with you." When she didn't answer, he murmured, "Oh, El."

She pulled her pink-and-green-striped scarf tighter around her neck, chewing on its itchy wool. She felt as if she were slowly fusing bone and blood, drowning in terror and the loneliness of being with only him. She was thinking to herself, *This would be a really stupid way to die. It's almost spring.* She was jealous of Jim's carefree nature. She wished she could feel euphoric when presented with the vastness of the sky, or the silence you can only find in nature. The forest wasn't for her. Or any woman, she reasoned. It was a setting for horror stories, for bodies buried in shallow dirt, for cougars to grab you from behind.

Jim inhaled again, leaned his head back. His black curls were dusted with snow. Jim was possibly the most handsome man Eleanor had ever dated. Relax, she commanded herself. She didn't want to be a man, but she wanted to be able to stand still in the darkness and feel neutral to fine. Goddammit, be in this moment. She shivered, popped open her mouth to free the soggy scarf. She tried to emulate his blithe stance. She failed.

Instead, she reached for the zipper of his worn-in 501s, startling him out of his moment of natural euphoria. She felt sturdier on the ice once her knees were planted firm, the relief of feeling momentarily embodied. He grinned through his surprise, still looking up at the moon. Oh, El.

Jim could never predict when they would have sex. If he initiated, she turned him down. Always. He learned to feign lack of interest, to never appear wanting, and there she would be, cold pink lips working him on a frozen pond. Or in the parking lot of the A&P, discussing when the Soviet Union became Russia again, when she shoved his hand violently under her skirt, grabbing him by the neck, demanding hard. Now. He learned to just roll with that feeling of shock and bewilderment. It started to be a turn-on. From one moment to the next, he never knew what could happen.

She liked it when he ejaculated on her breasts, and even now, in the cold, she ripped two buttons off her coat and pulled up her T-shirt so it could land hot against her skin. That single feeling, she told him, was almost enough to get her off.

The first time she asked him to, he said, "That's so porno," and laughed the way he did when he was uncomfortable. When she insisted, his forehead furrowed, like he couldn't believe a girl was making that request. The sex he'd had with Jennifer, his ex, had been nice, the way he thought sex was supposed to be. Jim considered himself a sweet guy, the kind who respected women. El pushed him to places he hadn't considered.

Eleanor demanded nakedness. She liked public places, awkward timing, the brash, obvious sleaze of sex. She liked the smell, and the weird way that human skin could look so weak. She liked how penises gave themselves away, rendered those attached to them so needy. Sex was ugly. It was always humiliating, no matter how romantic the moon, the setting. "Humans are just fucking gross," she said once, watching two conventionally attractive teenagers paw at each other in a bus shelter. "But remember how it felt, when it was all so new?" Jim said.

After Jim came, he laughed as though someone had said something absurd. He reached out to hold her, but she took a step back. She mashed her T-shirt against her chest, making a circle with her hand. Somehow the silence had grown more pronounced, the oblivion more sinister. She pulled her coat tight, turned and walked toward the fracture in the forest.

"Wait, I have a bottle of wine," Jim called after her. "I thought we could have a toast!"

"I'm fucking freezing." She flipped open her cellphone and tried to find the path in the faint blue light.

"Hold on, babe, I'll help you." Jim had a flashlight in his jean jacket pocket. He aimed the beam around her. He was always grateful after a blow job, like she'd just washed his floors or made him his favorite meal. She found his appreciation embarrassing, and it was partly why she liked to do it, to swing the balance of power in her favor. She didn't have the kind of emotional capacity that would allow her to wonder if he was feeling an intimate connection or closeness and she was reading his behavior cynically. She wouldn't even know what to do with those concepts. Attachment wasn't the goal.

⸺

When they got back in the car, Jim put the unopened bottle of wine in the trunk and pulled out a blanket to drape over Eleanor's legs; the car's heater was prone to shutting off for no reason. Eleanor pretended to fall asleep while he drove back to the city.

When the suburbs started clotting the view, and the glow of the cityline became a concrete visual, Eleanor's heart slowed.

"Honey, let's move to the country. Wouldn't it be wonderful to raise our kids there? Without all this bullshit?"

Eleanor's eyes grazed the skyline, now a row of ugly strip-mall-style, one-story roti shops and Naughty Vixen sex stores. "Sometimes, Jim, I think you've never listened to a single thing I've ever said besides *come on my tits*."

Although El had to admit to herself that, if anything, Jim listened almost too intently. He seemed to remember every detail of every story she ever told him. Lately, she'd been finding his attention irritating. Whenever she acted mean, she felt terrible, but she had no idea how to stop. The other day, her sister had said, "Jim is way too good for you. You better not fuck it up." El bristled, but knew her sister was right. She didn't want to be a mean person. She cared for Jim. It was as though she was incapable of taking that care and telling her mouth to stop ruining it.

Jim slowed at a stoplight and turned toward her. He looked hurt. El mumbled a stuttering, unconvincing apology. "I just don't feel safe in rural areas. I'm a city girl."

He nodded. "Of course, I knew that. It was stupid of me to suggest it."

They drove in silence. El contemplated the space between who she wanted to be and who she really was. She pulled off her scarf and balled it up, rubbing her neck. She felt the skin behind her ears, raised in a red-dotted rash from her allergy to wool.

Jim and Eleanor started dating last June, sort of. They were colleagues at a company called the Learning Caravan that bused amateur actors to elementary schools, where they'd perform experiments for the kids. Their slogan was "We Make Science Out of This World!" Eleanor had to wear a bug costume. Jim was on the science side, in charge of the chemicals. They were sponsored in part by the government and in part by a pharmaceutical conglomerate. The Learning Caravan traveled to Maine for a five-day tour of rural schools. The performers were either booked two to a room in Super 8 motels with carpets that felt like Rice Krispies squares or they'd stay with parents or teachers associated with the schools.

One night, when her sleeping options were either a basement pullout couch or a lounge chair, Eleanor opted to camp out in the van instead. So did Jim. They walked toward the van at the same time, lights in the windows of the house dimmed or shutting off. The sound of the highway nearby whirring.

"You forget something?" Eleanor asked as she slumped into the backseat and stretched out her legs.

Jim poked his head through the passenger-side door. "I was actually thinking of crashing here, you know. That house was odd."

Eleanor pushed the seats down to form a flat surface and makeshift bed. "There's room for both of us, I guess." When Jim lay down next to her, he was instantly turned on, and she noticed. Then he turned away.

For a few moments, Eleanor considered her options. Eleanor wasn't the kind of girl who turned heads, but her body moved as if she didn't give a fuck. She wouldn't sleep well thinking of how close they were, and how he had a hard-on. Maybe he would jerk off surreptitiously while she slept, and that grossed her out.

He didn't stop her when she reached around his curled body and placed her hand down into his jogging pants. She rolled him onto his back and held her free hand on his chest in a starfish and he found it hard to breathe. Just when he was about to come, she'd said, "Don't." She unzipped her jeans and said, "Watch me."

Jim didn't even remember Jennifer, their dog, their two-bedroom apartment overlooking the park, until hours later. Eleanor fell asleep fast, and he watched her until the sun crested the low hills behind the highway. In the morning, Jim felt a confusing mix of guilt and arousal, and the less El looked him in the eye, the more his obsession grew.

———

Almost a full year after that first encounter, and two months after Jim took Eleanor to look at stars in the country, they sat across from each other in the Dunkin' Donuts. Jim ate an apple fritter. El sipped a black coffee. She chewed the lip of the white cup. They had just had sex in the back of the number 32 bus. They had to go pick up their final paychecks from the Learning Caravan, which was going on hiatus for the summer. Jim was going to work for his dad at the tractor store. Eleanor was going to shampoo heads. They were both signed up to go back to the Caravan in the fall, but secretly hoped they'd find something better in the meantime.

"How long have you felt this way?" El asked.

"I dunno. A few weeks."

Through the window, El watched an old boyfriend saunter by and wave, holding his wife's hand. She remembered how he had always said "nice girl" and petted her head like a dog after sex.

"Jennifer was always so kind to me," Jim was saying. "I just feel like I was so awful to her, and had this thing with you— I can't even call it a relationship. I used to think I could make you fall in love with me, but it's mostly sexual, right? You're mean to me, and this is going to sound so weird, but it's like I almost enjoy it. It's not right. I'm not that guy."

El snorted, rolled her eyes, sipped her coffee. She made a point of looking at a sad fifty-plus couple sitting at an adjacent table. They were sharing a Boston cream doughnut, eating with plastic spoons, not talking. "You had sex with me because you are too weak," she said, watching the couple, "and then you had to break up with Jennifer because you are too honest. And then you got stuck with me." It was happening again. She felt like one of those tiny birds with mouths agape, waiting.

When Jim looked at her, he saw one of those mean cats, the ones that swipe at you and won't ever make eye contact.

"I fell in love with you, El," he said. "But I feel like, half the time, you don't even really like me."

Eleanor shrugged. A tear formed in the corner of her eye and she wiped it away. "How long have you been speaking to her?"

"Jenny? I don't know." He pretended to count backward, as if he didn't know precisely. "A few weeks now, I guess. We ran into each other at Costco." Of course. Costco. "It seems like she's forgiven me, you know, already. She was with a guy, and it made me so jealous. We started emailing and talking through our breakup and I just remembered all these good things about us. And, I guess, so did she."

Eleanor sighed.

"I still feel like I'm infatuated with you, you know, even though you make me feel so terrible about myself."

"I make you feel terrible about yourself?"

"Sometimes. I feel like your dog."

Eleanor snorted again. "That's rich. You cheat on me because"—she singsonged—"I make you feel bad about yourself."

"I didn't cheat on you. Jennifer and I are just talking."

"About getting back together?"

"I suppose."

Eleanor stood up and walked over to the garbage. She crumpled her coffee cup through one of the swinging doors.

Jim looked down and followed her. They pushed through the glass doors, then stood by the side of the parking lot.

Jim grabbed El's hand. "Oh, El." He started to cry.

It made Eleanor almost grateful, to pity him in that moment. When he just stood still with a normal, not-crying face, she could remember how much she loved having sex with him—even how much she looked forward to seeing him explain chemistry to the kids. He joked around onstage. The kids loved him. Their faces made El love him too, in those moments.

She watched him cry for a second, then said, "Okay, later. No use dragging this out." She walked toward the bus stop, knowing all Jim wanted was for her to admit that she'd miss him. Wanted her to cry. *No fucking dice,* she thought.

She went home and dragged her old dresser out onto the back porch and started stripping the years of paint from its wood. She took a shower, and then made her sister a lasagna. She did three loads of whites and dusted the bookshelves. When there was nothing left to do, she went down into her basement bedroom, cried, fell asleep, and didn't get up for fourteen hours.

———

By the second day at her new job, El actually missed wearing the bug costume. Teaching children about insects was a lot more fun than listening to women chat all day about the minutiae of their lives while she shampooed their heads and set them beneath the alien-like bubble of the hair dryer.

El's sister had set her up with the job, because she was one of the salon owners. "It's really not for you," she'd said. "You have to like people. And you're like Dad. You hate most people."

"I do not."

"El, it's so obvious."

Eleanor didn't like this assessment. She didn't want to be an antisocial person who didn't care for others. It wasn't what was in her heart. She just had this itchy impatience when they were too soft and loud and present. She wanted to feel what other people seemed to feel when presented with the warmth of a hug hello, a hearty "How you been?"

In September, the science crew reunited in a suburban mall parking lot on the side of a highway. Eleanor held a hard-shell, baby-blue suitcase from the 1970s that had once belonged to her dead mother. She wanted to scratch at her breasts because they were itchy under the push-up bra. She'd never worn one before. They were going to Virginia for four days. Eleanor convinced herself she'd get a lot of schoolwork done in her off-time and would ignore Jim completely. This year she was going to actually try to get good grades instead of just pass.

Aside from Jim, those employed by the Learning Caravan were not attractive folk. Eleanor was no exception: plain-faced, knock-kneed, bad skin, lusterless brown hair. But she now sported red highlights and pink nails; the girls at the salon had used her as a mannequin when it was slow. El was so starved for physical contact that she let them, felt soothed by their hands pulling at her hair, squeezing her shoulders when they turned the chair around so she could see the results in the mirror. Everyone from the science crew kept complimenting her new hair. She felt awkward.

Jennifer drove Jim to the parking lot and stood next to him while he loaded his gear into the side compartment of the yellow converted school bus. Neither of them looked at Eleanor.

Jennifer looked just like Eleanor imagined. Clean-cut, tapered jeans, a homely sweatshirt with a brand name across the breasts. She could be a Sunday school teacher. Like she waited until prom to have sex.

Eleanor learned about sex when she was twelve. Her sister brought boys home after school, and their apartment was small. El would study in the kitchen while her sister had sex on the couch. She grew to despise the way her sister would just lie there. Afterward El would ask, "What does it feel like?"

Her sister would shrug. "Kind of painful and awkward, but I like having a boyfriend."

The first time Eleanor got felt up, she was fourteen. Her lab partner, Alan, with the bad part in his hair and a laugh like a handful of shaking change, was over at the apartment. They were studying for a physics test, and El wasn't sure what came over her. She said, "You wanna see my tits?" She stood up in front of the shelf of debate trophies in her small bedroom.

Alan was instantly covered in sweat and looked as though he might throw up. But he nodded. El took off her shirt. Alan stared at her. He looked lobotomized. El found herself smiling. She liked the way Alan looked, as if his brain had emptied, when not five minutes earlier he was boasting about how much he knew about atmospheric pressure.

She walked over to him and put her right breast in his mouth. Alan made a yelping sound like a seal she'd seen at the aquarium, jerked up and ran out the door. That night, Eleanor moved her hand fast under the covers until it went numb. She pictured a shirtless teen TV star lying on his back, her right foot pinning his chest to the floor, his eyes wide and frightened, watching her.

Jim and Eleanor sat at opposite ends of the bus while they caught up with their colleagues. They performed at three schools back to back and arrived at a highway-side motel exhausted. Nobody at the Learning Caravan knew that El and Jim had broken up, so the coordinator had booked them a room together. Jim asked around, but no one wanted to switch.

Jim made a show of laying out his sleeping bag flat on the floor, even though the bed was ample and they'd shared one a thousand times. He went outside and called Jennifer from his cell. Eleanor could hear him through the window, lying, saying he was bunking with Todd, the audiovisual coordinator.

That night, Eleanor sat on the bed reading. Jim pretended to sleep.

Eventually, Eleanor said, "I can't sleep. Do you want to have a drink? Like, just as friends?"

Jim sat up in the dark. "Okay."

They went to the corner store and bought a case of beer. They drank the first few silently, then they started going over their summers.

"Is everything good with Jenny?" Eleanor didn't really want to know the answer.

Jim shrugged. "Yeah, it's good. I mean, except she watches me all the time. She reads my email. I have to text her every five minutes. She begged me not to take this job again, but I really hated working at the shop." Eleanor was silent. "I guess I'm kind of happy to have some space for the whole week," Jim said. "I haven't been alone in quite a while."

Eleanor watched him as he spoke. She wanted to push him onto the ground and grind her hips into him. But it wasn't right. Now that she'd seen Jennifer, she couldn't do it. She didn't like the reversal of power, how Jim looked at her so casually.

"I've missed you," Jim offered.

"I've missed you too."

"You seem different, El."

"How?"

Jim shrugged. "Softer."

"It's the hair. I'm trying this new . . . feminine thing." El almost laughed.

After his third beer, Jim stood up, El presumed, to go to the bathroom. Instead, he walked over to where El was sitting cross-legged on the bed and kissed her hard on the mouth.

She was startled by it, but didn't push him away like she normally would have.

He stared at her. Then he took off his clothes and stood naked with a big grin on his face.

"Now it's your turn."

El giggled. She started to take off her clothes, throwing them in a pile on top of her nearby suitcase. Jim pulled back the sheets on the bed and got in.

"Turn around," Jim said. "Lie sideways."

Eleanor raised her eyebrows at him.

"Just do it," he said, smiling.

She lay sideways on the bed, head propped on the pillow. Jim curled around her body in a spoon, his hands clasped together around her waist. He kissed the back of her neck softly for a second, and then stopped.

El lay very still, unsure of what to do. She knew exactly what she would have done in the past, but decided not to try anything. After the digital alarm clock went from 1:02 to 1:08, she said, very quietly, "Jim?"

His breathing was slow and warm on her neck, and she realized he was fast asleep.

On her list of sexual conquests, Eleanor could not remember sleeping in a spoon with anyone, naked, ever. Eleanor shunned cuddling as a form of slow, forced strangulation. But this felt different. She contemplated moving his arm, but it felt so warm. Eventually, she stopped questioning it. They slept, curled in a half moon, until morning.

A PATCH OF BRIGHT FLOWERS

Julia is in a hotel room in Vancouver trying on a short dress. The skirt is creased with two wrinkles across the front as though she's crossed herself out. She insists on bringing only one piece of carry-on luggage no matter how long the tour. Still, she hopes the dress will get the attention of Bridie Heller, a woman she knows only from waxy back-flap author photos on the books assigned in college literature courses. That night there will be a welcome dinner for the authors participating in the literary festival, and Julia thinks that Bridie will be a great distraction from the mundanity of small talk and self-promotion. It will be a challenge, but Julia likes a challenge. She leafs through the festival brochure and notes that there are only three queer authors at this festival and only two are out—Julia and her friend Michael.

She files her nails and paints them as gray as the sky while watching a cable show about jungle cats.

To wrestle up her courage, Julia empties a tiny bottle of mini-bar Scotch into a plastic hotel cup still encased with the cellophane wrapper because her nails are too wet to rip it open. Julia likes immediacy. The Scotch burns. She coughs.

The dress is too big in the tits and shows a little too much back, which wouldn't be a problem if she didn't have the lyrics to a Nirvana song connecting her shoulder blades. Julia has been thinking about covering it up with a patch of bright flowers but noted during the previous year's Pride festivities that every femme over thirty-two has some nineties tribal Celtic armband or women's symbols covered up by patches of pansies. She didn't want to stand among the unified flower beds, slowly wrinkling under inky gardens.

Julia isn't sure what to do about aging. She loves that queers are granted an extended adolescence, and aren't really expecting to marry, have babies, or own property until they are well into their thirties. If at all. Everyone is buzzing about Obama's recent victory but doesn't think gay marriage is going to happen for the whole country anytime soon. It had been legalized in Canada only a few years ago. She used to see ugly babies or annoying children and think, *Oh thank god I'm not a parent. Thank god I can do whatever I want, whenever I want.* Recently, whenever she sees an ugly baby, she thinks, *I would love that little monster SO HARD.* The freedom has begun to feel like its own form of constraint.

Julia presses two pearls of moisturizing cream under each eye and smooths them out. She forgot to bring mascara. She'd packed in a hurry, with a hangover, after a marathon fight with her girlfriend. Julia has just turned thirty-five and is now certain, without a doubt, that she wants to have a baby. Her girlfriend, also thirty-five, is suddenly certain she does not. They are at a stalemate. So they fight about who cleaned the toaster oven crumb tray, and who steals the blanket every night, and things they can see and quantify. When they got a little tipsy a few weeks ago, Julia said, "Now that marriage is legal, have you thought about proposing?" Her girlfriend admitted yes, but it didn't feel like the right time. Julia said, "*Same*." It wasn't even a sad moment, just quietly factual. For Julia, the tour of hotels and incessant chitchat with readers and other writers could not have come at a better time.

Julia and her girlfriend have an arrangement for travel. The basic rule is: when you are on the road, your body is your own. Although they are not permitted to sleep with anyone who currently lives in their city or is planning to relocate there anytime soon.

When she checked into the hotel an hour earlier, she'd glanced around the author hospitality room and knew that her attempts to dress the part of a classy novelist were going to fail. She felt perennially covered in cat fur, a walking visual flaw. Scrawling her signature on the sign-in list, she noted coffee stains on the front of her spring coat. It was a coat she bought after deciding to stop layering her body in hoodies and instead accept her age in something tailored.

Her feet were soaking wet from the rain she always thought was a regional exaggeration. A girl with a shiny red bob handed her a festival guide and an envelope of per diem cash. "I really loved your book. Really. I could really see my world in it," she said. Julia felt a rush of gratitude toward this young woman and stopped herself from complaining about the review she'd read on the plane that called the book "a tawdry, sex-crazed tale of emotionally shallow, drug-addicted, gender-confused lowlifes no one could ever love enough to care about seeing through to the end of the book." The world was full of petty assholes, she thought.

Julia said thank you, and the girl smiled, offering her a festival tote bag. Julia decided to fix herself a coffee while she waited until her hotel room was ready.

Every literary festival manages to bring in that one author who is mind-blastingly famous. Someone who can guarantee the audiences are filled with both book lovers and those who only read one novel a year. And sure enough, at a table in the corner, the Famous One was holding court, signing copies of a new science fiction book she refused to call science fiction. A fawning festival organizer picked up each copy after she signed it and placed it on the table in a stack, running her palm over the covers as if to soothe them from nerves.

When the Famous One got up and approached the refreshments table, Julia tried to project an air of *who cares about you*, but her hands shook when she was pouring milk into her mug, and when she leaned over to reach for a spoon, Julia's plasticized name tag swung on its lanyard and dipped into the sugar bowl. The Famous One stirred her coffee, looking down into the cup. Some women just looked classy all the time. For the Famous One, Julia decided, it was all about her shoes. And the way she never hurried. That magic combination.

Julia, on the other hand, is always in a rush to do things, and to do too many things at once—and she is often getting into accidents. She starts to do something and then remembers she wants to do something else, so she stops in mid-action to take another action, and then she falls or trips or stumbles. Julia is trying to follow through more, in life and relationships and sentences and up and down stairs. She thinks it's working; she has fewer scrapes and bruises, fewer broken heels.

At home, Julia tends bar on the weekends and writes on

weekdays. At festivals, she often feels as though she'd be more comfortable hanging with the catering staff than standing making chitchat with the latest literary award winner. She thought about telling the Famous One how much she loved her books, but though it would have been a way in, it wouldn't have been true. Instead, she took a hurried gulp of her coffee and wished her room was ready. Julia loves hotels. They still feel like a new thing, an exciting thing, a symbol. The hotel is her favorite part of a book tour, that feeling as if you are eight and living in a fort of couch cushions, a tiny little world away from routine.

It was then, as she stood awkwardly beside her carry-on suitcase, that she saw Bridie Heller for the very first time. Well, she had no idea she was The Bridie Heller. Bridie had the telltale swagger of an old-school butch, moving gently about the room filled with sixty-something boomer writers, twenty-something assistants, forty-something publicists, the Famous One, and Julia, the lone thirty-five-year-old invited to the festival for a "voice of the young" panel discussion. The other two "young" ones, who Julia knows to be thirty-nine and forty-one, respectively, were arriving tomorrow.

Julia is in denial about being thirty-five. The week before, she'd stood in line at a bar in the west end of Toronto for their weekly lesbian night. A twenty-two-year-old hipster in front of her had said to her friend, "If I'm still standing in lines like this when I'm thirty, just shoot me." A friend three years younger complained about needing to have a baby before thirty-five, when her chances would drop significantly. Julia loves that she is still considered young in this milieu. She doesn't want to hear about fertility treatments. She just wishes time had paused at twenty-eight, and she could give her girlfriend more time to think about it. She could have a savings account, and own furniture that wasn't secondhand. If they got married now, they probably couldn't afford a reception that wasn't potluck.

Bridie walked by Julia, who was still standing by the refreshments table sipping her coffee, leaning on her suitcase trolley, trying to convey with every muscle in her body and expression on her face, *Hello hello you're not the only queer in the room hi hi hi hi hi hi*. She cursed her decision to wear slouchy jeans for the purposes of airplane comfort.

Julia willed Bridie to look at her, make eye contact, but she didn't. Julia took exaggerated notice of Bridie's name tag, pinned above her shirt pocket, where she kept a neatly folded handkerchief. Julia loved that hankie immediately. Finally, Julia forced a note of brightness into her voice and said, "Bridie!"

Bridie looked up from her small white plate of melon chunks and said, "Hello," giving that smile that people use when they assume you've met before but they clearly can't place you.

"I love your work. I'm Julia Chapman." This was a lie. Bridie wrote the kind of novels that Julia often gave to her mother for Christmas. Generational sagas about torn-apart families, often involving a nineteenth-century across-the-ocean move and some sort of tragic secret. Nothing set after the 1960s or involving even the most minimal of gay side characters. Nary a matronly spinster auntie or a flamboyant and "single" hairdresser. That Bridie Heller was actually a savvy butch you'd expect to see at the local lez bar playing pool with some gender studies femme professor for a wife was totally confounding.

"Thank you," said Bridie, who pointed toward the cork-board behind Julia that featured media clippings about authors attending the festival. "You've certainly been getting some great press," she said, pointing to a giant photo of Julia from the *Vancouver Sun*, the headline reading YOUNG AUTHOR IS UNAFRAID TO WRITE OF QUEER WORLDS. Bridie smirked at the headline, seemed embarrassed. She didn't say anything nice, like "I hope to read it soon" or any of the other potential half-truths writers tell each other. Her eyes seemed to be mocking her, something that Julia had encountered before. Like what she writes about are things only a few select people care about. Like her books won't be shortlisted for awards and are not considered important literature. Julia tries not to care about those things, and thinks, instead, about her readers, and the writers who inspired her to keep going. But it nags at her, that she is some sort of imposter, allowed into the party of legitimate artists only as a clown, a form of amusement, producing work that could never be canon. Maybe my work isn't even any good, she thinks at three in the morning, listening to the odd clicks and whirs in every new hotel room, getting up to check that the latch on her door is locked. If she doesn't go back to sleep, she becomes obsessed with listing off other things she could do for a living that might be as fulfilling.

Bridie's publicist arrived with her schedule. "Your room is ready."

Bridie seemed pleased for the reason to leave.

"Nice to meet you!" Julia said as the duo walked away, neither looking back.

Now Julia tries to safety-pin the dress under her right armpit. Eventually, her breasts look even. She remembers a time when she used to be called Perky, at age twenty-one when everything pointed skyward. When she leans into the mirror to line her eyes, the pin stabs her. "Fuck!" She sits back on the bed, marveling that she wrote something that actually allows her to be sitting in this hotel room free of charge. Success is still a great big shock and she doesn't always trust it.

By the third book, she had her rituals: wrap the remote control in a ziplock bag, pocket the shampoos if they were nice and ask for more. Always fill out the little thing on the door that allowed you to get breakfast delivered in the morning. Pack granola bars and dried fruit, and google the closest drugstore beforehand. Keep receipts for tax time.

When she was younger, her parents preferred camping trips. National parks and canoeing, hiking. An old canary-yellow tent. They stayed in a hotel only once, on the side of a highway, because it was storming too hard to pitch the tent in a nearby campground. Her mother made them eat hot dogs that had been cooked in the hotel coffee maker and wrapped in white bread. A part of Julia still thinks that staying at hotels where you don't park your car in front of your room means something good about her career.

Until she published her first book, Julia had never taken a trip, really. The odd jaunt to Montreal or Ottawa, places she could go to for a weekend. She'd never been on a plane until her publicist said, "Okay, so here's your ticket, and someone named Gail will meet you at the airport."

When she'd met Gail, a woman in her sixties holding a sign with her name, Julia couldn't stop talking about the flight. "I thought I might throw up. I was so scared!" The woman looked a little pained after a while, driving fast in her blue Subaru toward Granville Island. "You look so young," Gail said to her, over and over. "I can't believe you've written a book."

"Thanks," Julia said. She had no idea then that she was going to have to get used to this kind of remark, and that it wasn't always a compliment.

Back in her hometown, when her cousin Anna found out she'd published a book of poetry, she assumed Julia had immediately become rich. Anna stole two sweaters from her suitcase, later telling her mother, "Well, she can afford to buy new ones, right?" But Julia's life hadn't changed at all. In fact, she had even less money. She stopped going home so much.

At the dinner, Julia is seated between her publicist and Michael, a gay poet from Alberta she very much admires. The seat across from her is empty until the end of the appetizer course, when she looks up from her plate of asparagus to see Bridie Heller.

Bridie Heller is no longer someone she might flirt with to pass the time, to feel better about her failing relationship at home. No. Bridie Heller is a seduction challenge. Because Bridie Heller is charming and interested in chatting with everyone except Julia. And the only thing Julia likes more than immediate gratification is the kind that comes after a very serious game, requiring cunning and hair twirling and her very best efforts.

During dinner, the Famous One talks about the 1970s and how poets would spend months in France writing on the grant council's dime, or living together in a cabin outside Toronto, and all the authors who'd become famous and died. They are colorful anecdotes, and Julia wishes she could go back and watch the poets scrapping drunkenly. "But you know what he was like," says the Famous One, and everyone laughs. Julia nods, sipping her wine. Bridie tells her own stories to nearby companions in a low voice.

After dinner, Julia follows the crowd to the reading where Bridie Heller is a featured guest. She reads in a slow, low monotone, and if Julia hadn't established her personal challenge, she would've drifted off or gone for a cigarette midway through. Like straight women who come on to lesbians on book tours, Julia regards cigarettes as an out-of-context exception. She considers herself a nonsmoker and won't touch one when she gets home, but on tour . . . well, things just don't count. She buys a hardcover of Bridie Heller's book and gets in line to have it signed.

The wait is more than fifteen minutes, and when Julia finally reaches the signing table, she leans over and proffers the creamy off-white title page. Bridie scrawls *Best Wishes, Bridie Heller.*

Cheap, thinks Julia. When Bridie looks up at Julia's raised eyebrows, she winks and says, "Thanks for buying the book."

Though Julia wants to go back to her room and order food and watch cable TV, she goes to the hospitality suite to wait for Bridie. She eats a dinner of triangle-shaped crackers, cheese cubes, and cucumber slices, while discussing why prose poetry is out of fashion, how one of the biggest prize-winners in Canada is cheating on his wife with a publisher and everyone knows but the wife, who is also an author albeit not as prolific. When Julia says, "Why do these men insist on monogamy when they know they'll fail?" she is met with appalled silence and excuses herself to refresh her drink. There she bumps into Bridie, who is drinking Scotch from a plastic cup and somehow making it look sophisticated and masculine.

Bridie has taken notice of Julia's obvious intentions and seems bored enough to play along. Eventually, when the rest of the crowd is immersed in a never-ending, soul-deadening debate about the advent of e-books and the death of the publishing industry, Bridie asks, "Do you smoke?"

And Julia replies, "Yes, because it doesn't count. On book tour, they're fictional."

"What?"

"When I'm on a book tour, the cigarettes are imagined. I quit two years ago."

Bridie doesn't think this is clever or interesting, just pulls out a pack of smokes from her front pocket and walks down the hallway ahead of Julia, as Julia struggles to keep up in her too-tall heels.

Bridie makes her nervous, she realizes. *So nervous I have no game at all.*

Bridie pauses at the door and holds it open for Julia. They stand near two oversized potted plants and stare out at the ocean. The sun is going down and the water is dotted with taxi boats going downtown. Julia wonders aloud if she could live in Vancouver or if the rain would kill her. Bridie replies that she spent several years here after university. They continue to make small talk—how many other cities are you going to, who is your agent, did you hear about so-and-so's six-figure advance, et cetera. The setting is romantic, but Julia can't stop herself from continuing to talk business when she should at least be talking about art or ideas or anything she can normally talk about with ease. She traces her finger along the tattoo of Kathy Acker on her inner right wrist, while still discussing book advances. *I didn't used to be this boring.*

There is a pause, and Julia thinks she might tunnel into the ground from embarrassment, until Bridie says, "So, what is your deal?"

"My deal?"

"Yes."

"I dunno, I think you're interesting."

"You do?"

"Yes." Then Julia, feeling the free champagne crowd her better judgment, says, "I'm excited to read your new book." She rationalizes this could be true eventually.

"Do you remember writing a review about five years ago of my third book, *The Ghost's Garden*?"

Julia's cheeks redden. The safety pin jabs her right armpit. She remembers it vaguely, a short review she wrote for an arts weekly and, from the look on Bridie's face, she gathers a not very positive one.

"Should I apologize?"

"No. I believe in critical reviews, but I think yours was lazy."

"Probably. I got paid about three cents an hour to write those."

Julia and Bridie stare at each other, as though in a standoff. All around them other hotel patrons mill about, flipping open their phones and lighting cigarettes, getting in and out of taxis. People nod at Bridie. She nods back. Julia absorbs the fact that Bridie's aloofness wasn't about Julia being young or annoying or uncool, it was because she'd written a bad review of her book. Julia knows the names of all her bad reviewers. She is horrified to be on Bridie's list. But she still wants to win this challenge.

"So, do you have a wife?" asks Julia.

"Not really."

"What does that mean?"

"We are still living together, but we are not really together anymore. When marriage became legal, we didn't believe in it enough to, you know, actually get it done."

"Same, for me and my girlfriend."

"So, you're not single?"

"I'm single here."

Bridie nods. Julia appreciates that she never has to explain this arrangement to other queer people.

"You smirk a lot," says Bridie.

Julia stops smirking. "I smile sometimes when I'm uncomfortable."

"It comes off as snobby."

"Well, that's certainly not my intention."

"You're so sarcastic, it's hard to know when you're being real. Like, following me around all night, is that real? Your generation—"

"Oh, I always love sentences that begin with 'Your generation.'"

"—is so cynical, it's like there's no beauty to anything you can't mock. It's like there are quotation marks around every action you make."

"That's a ridiculous reduction. How do you even know my age?"

"What, you're twenty-six?"

"Thirty-five."

Bridie raises her eyebrows. "Really? I'd assumed, because . . ."

"You'd never heard of me until this book, so you think I'm in my twenties?"

"Well, yes."

"It's my seventh."

"I didn't know you had other books."

"It's my first published by a—"

"A multinational, yes. Your main character is twenty-one, it's written in first person, I'd assumed it was autobiographical." Bridie blushes, shrugs. "I guess I should apologize now."

"And you are, what? Forty-five?"

"Fifty."

"A hot fifty."

Bridie smiles. Her shoulders relax, a blush creeps into her face.

Bingo, thinks Julia. She wonders if Bridie is a top. "So, what is it really that you're criticizing, Obi-Wan?"

Bridie smirks this time. Inhales her cigarette, not breaking eye contact.

"Your characters are younger."

"I like writing about young people. Your characters are all, what, two hundred thirty-six years old?"

"I'm a historian. We're already saturated in the present. I like to write stories that provide an escape from the tyranny of this day and age."

"The tyranny of what? Being un-closeted?"

"I love that you assume I'm closeted."

"Aren't you? You never write about it. You never mention your wife in the media. I bet your publicist makes reporters promise not to ask about it."

"Look at me, Julia. It's obvious to anyone with sight that I am who I am. I'm a very private person. My personal life is my own."

"So is mine, but it doesn't mean I have to be dishonest."

"Your life might be honest, but it's incredibly public. I googled you and found out you ate pretzels on the plane yesterday, had a hangover, and are currently writing a script version of your first novel. Your cat's name is Binkie, you really like Mary Gaitskill, and you live with your long-term girlfriend in Parkdale."

Julia tries to appear calm. All she can hear is her inner monologue voice yelling, SHE GOOGLED ME! She recovers quick enough.

"So you know all about me. But who are you?"

"Yes, I do. But unlike me, you can easily blend in."

"Yes, the femme blend, such credible social commentary." Julia rolls her eyes at that one. "Anyway, it's not obvious to your readers. It's important for people to have role models."

"Oh god, if you give me the Think-about-the-gay-kids-in-Idaho speech, I take back my generational cynicism comment."

"But there's truth to that. I rarely see my queer worlds represented in art."

"Do you always have to see yourself? It's art, we don't write to make a political point. Didactic art reeks of inauthenticity, you can detect it from miles away."

"Is that what you think of my work?"

"I didn't say that. I actually think your work is good. You have a way with humor."

"Do I?"

"Oh, the writer ego. You're gonna keep pressing for compliments, aren't you?"

"Maybe."

"In that case, your dress is very distracting. In a good way."

They hold each other's gaze for a few seconds, long enough

for Julia to know Bridie is absolutely a top. Julia debates lean-ing in to kiss her, feels that charged energy between them, but just when she's about to move in, Bridie stubs her cigarette in the ashtray and walks back inside. Julia briefly wonders if she is imagining the energy between them. They return to the hospitality suite. For the next hour or so, Julia has several long conversations with other people, but keeps an eye on Bridie. She half pays attention to a lot of people, all of whom she should be networking with or getting to know because she might start invaluable friendships, but she can only see Bridie in her periphery. *She stands so well.* This is what she's thinking while pretending to listen to an author whose books she grew up adoring. She tries to keep it together but eventu-ally gives up and sips what she decides will be her last drink. She lingers by the door saying good night to others, and notes Bridie heading her way. They stand by the elevator, not speak-ing, and get off on the same floor.

When the elevator door opens, Bridie walks Julia to her door and they stand awkwardly in front of it for a moment. Bridie leans in and kisses Julia gently, and pulls away.

"You happy you caught me?"

"Yeah."

"I suppose, because of your girlfriend, you're not going to invite me in."

"Oh, I thought you understood me earlier. It's like book tour cigarettes," Julia says. "She's fictional."

"Your girlfriend is fictional?" Bridie says, narrowing her eyes.

"We have an arrangement for these kinds of things, for when we travel."

"Oh, okay. Well, good night, Julia Chapman, voice of a generation of narcissists."

"Good night, Bridie Heller, closet case for the Oprah's Book Club set . . ."

Bridie leans in and kisses Julia again. It's the kind of kiss that unravels something in her. Her inner monologue fades.

"You can't write about this," jokes Bridie, once they are inside the room and she has one hand on Julia's waist and the other on her neck. Caught.

"I wouldn't dream of it."

Julia smirks again, but it's an expression of quiet triumph.

The next morning, Bridie is gone. Julia showers and gets ready for an early-morning reading. As she walks toward the venue, gripping a coffee and a bashed-up reading copy of her novel, she sees Bridie get into a cab bound for the airport. They hold each other's gaze. Neither waves.

THIS IS CARRIE'S
WHOLE LIFE

When Carrie is alone with a stranger, she imagines how they might kill her. She used to think her imaginings were an evolutionary instinct, the body's way of creating the neural pathways required for the worst eventuality. But when someone really tried to kill her, she changed her mind. Her imagination hadn't prepared her at all. Now she knows her limbs are useless props, as worthless as daisy stems after a week in stale vase water.

Carrie is slicing limes with the good knife, the one that cuts clean. The knife stays sharp because Carrie wrote NO EFFING DISHWASHER on its handle with a Sharpie. She's listening to a mix labeled *Opening! Duties! at the Dark Hearse!* The bar is called the Dark Horse, but everyone who works there calls it the Hearse because eventually it makes you feel as though you're in one. If you consider what happened to

Carrie, that's pretty funny. Whoever made the list doesn't work there anymore.

Her nails are polished yellow like a child's crayon sun. She juts out one hip, sings along to a chorus of a song that is simply the word *Barcelona*. She throws the limes into their plastic tub, setting it beside the box of straws. She rinses the cutting board before walking it over to the dish pit. Elin is stacking pint glasses in the sterilizing machine. She wears a snapback and baggy shorts with a white tank top. The tattoos of finely illustrated rabbits up and down her right arm appear to be hopping on her flexing muscles.

Here, Carrie says.

Elin holds the cutting board and smirks.

Thanks, doll.

The sexual tension between them, if harnessed, could power the dishwasher.

A few weeks later, after the incident, Elin stops by Carrie's apartment with a stack of Jane Austen novels and a box of cinnamon doughnuts. Elin sits awkwardly on the end of her bed as Carrie tries to explain how she has always imagined being murdered every time she was alone with another human. She's only told a handful of people in her life about it. Elin is the first person who says, Oh yeah, me too. Of course. If I'm alone with any man, I imagine my murder.

Carrie is about to express how much this means to her when Elin stands up and says she has to split. When Carrie thanks her for saving her life, all she says is, It was nothing, you'd have done the same thing. Then she shows herself out.

She didn't try to kiss her. They only ever hook up at the bar in a way that feels mutually transactional, like they don't exist in each other's lives outside of work.

———

Isn't there some sort of Buddhist saying about admitting your human frailty? Or maybe it was from the corporate leadership book that Carrie's ex-boyfriend left on the back of the toilet. It was good to roll joints on.

This is Self-Help 101, she said during their last week together, but marketed to men.

That book changed my life, Carrie, he insisted. Why do you always have to mock me?

I'm not mocking you, I'm mocking this book, this author, the way men have to have anything emotional disguised as capitalistic advice.

If you think this book is stupid, you think I'm stupid.

She'd scoffed when he said this. He was being a baby. But later she realized she did say derisive things to him, often disguised as jokes. It was her sense of humor, she thought, the things that came naturally out of her mouth. She asked herself if she'd wanted to hurt his feelings. She did not. She would feel very protective if anyone else hurt his feelings. But the book *is really* self-help for men. Was it an insult? She was trying to say that men don't consume things regarded as feminine unless they're disguised. And that makes both the people who publish such books and those who consume them kind of stupid. Aren't I allowed to have an opinion about the book? Could she love someone who was influenced by such a ridiculous book?

As a child, Carrie loved the sidelines. She loved to play by herself, with a coterie of imaginary friends. She would have won a gold medal in daydreaming if it qualified for the Olympics. She loved longing and imagining and waiting. She hated being called on in class, playing dodgeball, and group projects. She had one best friend whom she loved fiercely, and when that friend moved to Arnprior in seventh grade, she replaced her with a boyfriend named Jeremy.

The book fight happened again, but this time, instead of a book, it was a person. A very agreeable woman her boyfriend worked with and whose company he enjoyed so much that when she met the woman, Carrie couldn't even be jealous. The woman laughed at things that were not funny, a giggle like a pause between clauses. When Carrie asked her opinion about the mayor of the city, the woman said she didn't think anything about the mayor. She said, with genuine sincerity, she loved reality shows about weddings. Carrie was jealous only of this woman's simplicity, not of her body or the way she was obviously sexually interested in her boyfriend. Imagine never thinking deeply. Imagine the bliss of that.

After they met, at a work function, her boyfriend said, You have nothing to worry about. At all. But she knew it wasn't true. She stayed late after work the next day and hooked up with Elin for the first time, making out in the back booth after singing a sloppy karaoke duet of "Islands in the Stream."

Now the woman and her ex-boyfriend are married and live in Newmarket in a house that looks like every other house on their street. The last message her ex sent her read *I miss our late night debates.*

—

After the breakup with her boyfriend, the murder daydreams get stronger. The last time Carrie involuntarily imagines someone killing her—before it actually happens—she is at Lucky Head, the salon she chose only because it was closest to her house. Her stylist, Emma, called in sick, so she meets her replacement, a small, chatty man named Alex, late on a Friday. The lazy winter sun sets at 4:30 P.M.; both of them are quiet as Queen Street glows pinky gray from the second-floor window. He sends the front desk assistant home. As he gently leans her head back into the sink and rinses the toner from her hair, she is aware of every small part of her face and neck, how he's touching the most sensitive parts of her body that keep her alive. People have had strokes from the neck pressure of those shampoo sinks. Something worse would be too easy. She continues to make small talk with Alex. The song playing is "Tainted Love." When Alex is finished, she tips 30 percent even though she doesn't love her haircut because she's relieved the appointment is over and she isn't dead. It is a blip in her thinking. A stuck key in her brain. She has nothing against Alex. If someone were to ask her to describe Alex, she would use adjectives like *gentle, sweet, lithe, breakable.*

The thought of being killed probably occurs to most women in the usual places—cabs, dark streets, elevators. When calling a plumber or a cable technician. And of course, on every first date. The funny thing is, Carrie doesn't think about it with Gregor because she has known him for over two years. Once she's known people for a long time, the imaginings stop. After Gregor tries to kill Carrie, she doesn't quit her job. She goes back for her next shift as though nothing has happened.

Gregor lives in an apartment above the bar with his wife. He's fifty-five but doesn't usually remember his exact age. It's hard to say if Gregor always lacked interiority or if alcohol dissolved it after several decades. He has never felt known, except briefly during his first few years of marriage when he and his wife ran a campground north of the city. He loved raking the beach every morning, and selling the firewood, and the looks on the kids' faces when they bought Popsicles and french fries from the truck in the middle of the property. Gregor and his wife had a small wooden cottage where they lived from May until after Labor Day.

Before the incident, he came in every night at 6 P.M. and stayed until ten or so, unless his wife came downstairs from the apartment and pulled him out right before *Jeopardy*. Why do you want to drink with the children? she'd say in a thick Hungarian accent, before looking at Carrie, helpless. It's true, Carrie's bar catered to people in their mid-twenties. The oldest patrons they'd get were an occasional table of thirty-somethings after work.

Gregor was balding, with a scruffy gray-and-white beard.

He always took the stool right in front of the cash register. Whenever Carrie settled up with a customer, they had to basically cuddle up to Gregor, who would tell them to tip big because Carrie had dreams. He always asked if he could help her slice limes, fold napkins, clean the menus. She'd refuse, and then he would tell her she was doing it wrong. It used to bother her, but eventually she was able to tune him out.

Now, as she checks the bottles of house wine in the small fridge under the bar, she hears his voice. But, of course, he's locked away.

He was generally a disgusting man, but his fingers were especially grotesque. Cracked, dirty half-moons. On Fridays he would bring in a stack of lottery tickets and scratch cards and busy himself. It reminded Carrie of when her niece Jessica turned seven and was finally able to entertain herself. On other nights he would monologue her to death. Carrie looked forward to Friday when the owner, an alcoholic named Penny, would show up. She loved Gregor. Always be nice to my guy here! she'd slur. Carrie couldn't tell if they really knew each other or if it was just the loyalty of one drunk recognizing another drunk.

It was sort of Carrie's fault, in a way. There was a wild rainstorm outside and it was a slow night. Penny didn't believe in having a bar TV: The point of bars is to communicate! Love one another! If Penny stayed until last call, she would end up kissing whoever was next to her at the bar—didn't matter who it was, as long as they were just as obliterated. It grossed Carrie out so much she had to turn away from the spectacle. She couldn't cut Penny off the way she did other customers, and when she watched Penny stumble into the street, she worried about being liable for whatever injury might befall her.

But they lost a lot of business without the TV. Every other bar was packed because it was World Cup time. Carrie decided to close early, locked the door, and went down to the basement to do the count. She didn't know Gregor was in the men's room. She came back upstairs to pour herself a whiskey and Coke before mopping up and there he was. His face was red. He was holding a jagged wine bottle that he'd grabbed from the wine fridge and then broken. He looked at Carrie as if it were her fault that his plan to steal a bottle of wine had failed.

WHY IS THE DOOR LOCKED? he screamed.

She tried to reply that the lock was just tricky even from the inside and required a key. But he was already lunging at her.

She didn't save herself. That was the worst thing. She always thought she would fight back. Then Elin came in the back door, like she often did when they agreed on a clandestine after-work hookup. She was a weird little skateboard kid, but the adrenalin made her able to pull Gregor off Carrie. Elin kicked Gregor in the face and restrained him on the ground while yelling at Siri to call 911.

When someone endangers their own life to save yours, it feels like being on drugs, Carrie thought, like you've been drugged to love them forever in a desperate way.

The strangest thing about the encounter—the experience of telling the cops, the hospital, the stitches in her side that got rubbery and white with time, the court case—is that Carrie didn't change her life. She didn't do anything on the lists she made on the back of receipts on Thursday nights, the ones with new life plans. Go back to school. Move to Vancouver. Community theater. Volunteer at the animal shelter. Call her friends more. Rent a new apartment, one with more light, above ground. She just kept going back to work. She kept fucking Elin on the cases of beer in the storeroom after last call. She even kept her hair the same. Eventually, Elin quit the bar, and Carrie started dating the new manager, Andrea. They moved in together. But that was the only thing that changed, really. She simply had the same life, alongside someone else; and, because Andrea got a better job and could buy a house, the objects around her were nicer—a couch that wasn't secondhand, a barbecue in a backyard, a shared leased Toyota, two duvet covers instead of one.

Knowing that she wasn't actually stuck in a rut, that she was choosing the mundanity of her life, did change her perspective, though. She no longer yearned to be different. She had survived this weird thing, a cut that, if it had been two centimeters to the left, would have killed her. She kept choosing to live her life in the same way. Maybe that wasn't a weakness. Maybe she was just opting out of the falseness of having bigger dreams and learning to be okay with it.

That's what she explained to the victims' rights therapist who was assigned to her case.

It sounds like you might be a bit numb, the therapist said.

Carrie considered this. Decided it wasn't true. No, I think I actually am fine. I think I live a fine life, she replied.

Are you happy?

I don't think humans actually want to be happy. I think that's a useless quest, really. A marketing thing. I think life is varying degrees of difficult and easy, and the easy times are nice, those little pleasures in a regular day. I think what happened was a gift, maybe.

Getting stabbed was a gift?

In a way, yes. I'm no longer dissatisfied. I'm just, like, awake and can see things clearly now.

In 2019, Andrea breaks up with her right before their seven-year anniversary. Andrea says, I need someone who is more present in this life. Who wants to be spontaneous! Who feels all the big things! Andrea writes a list of all the ways Carrie can't meet her needs. She reads them out loud to her. *I want someone who wants more than to work in a bar. I want someone who doesn't watch as much TV.* When Carrie just accepts this, Andrea gestures wildly, so everyone in the café stares. This is why! You have no reaction! I want a life of reactions! I'd rather you punch me in the face than just stare at me like that!

Carrie moves out of Andrea's house and rents a basement apartment. She half unpacks her belongings, and then she has a nervous breakdown. She didn't realize that Andrea's mere presence, the way she ordered the world and kept the days moving, was keeping her together. All her life she has seen breakdowns onscreen as cinematic, an intense cre-scendo. There is a lot of screaming and crying and self-harm. There is often a break with reality. Most of all, people in the person's life rally around them. They wrap them in scarves and put them in midsize Volvos and drive them to hospital wards that are often in the country. They bring them food warmed in casserole dishes and make them go for walks. In real life, this doesn't happen. Or if it does, it's the exception.

For Carrie, it is different. She doesn't realize she is having a nervous breakdown until it is too late. The same way women often die of heart attacks, assuming it is indigestion; they just go to sleep and never wake up. Carrie's breakdown starts as a deep, unwavering feeling of solitude. Like mental hypothermia, slowly shutting down her system. She stops things slowly. At first, she stops going to the gym because the pandemic shuts them down, and then she doesn't go back when they reopen. Then she stops meeting friends for dinner in their yards, on their porches, in the park. Then her roommate moves out and she doesn't try to find a new one. She doesn't go home for the holidays. She doesn't go to the movies anymore. She gets her first vaccine and then the follow-up. When the lockdown lifts, she goes to work but starts to call in sick. She doesn't go to the grocery store, she orders delivery. Food expires and she doesn't replace it. She doesn't go to the door to collect the mail. She eats spoonfuls of coffee whitener and raw noodles and water from an old plastic cup. She doesn't go to the bathroom to brush her teeth.

She just stops.

She sends one text, to Andrea: *I don't know what to do.*

Andrea says, *I don't know how to help you.*

She calls Elin, who answers—in Los Angeles, where she's become a celebrity photographer—but Elin doesn't know what to say besides you're going to be okay.

Carrie knows she won't be.

Elin texts an hour later asking if she wants to go to the hospital. *I could stay on the phone with you if you call a cab.*

Carrie briefly imagines being trapped in a building overrun by COVID. *No*, she writes back. She then laughs at the irony, that she'll avoid a hospital so she doesn't catch a fatal disease, but she might die because of that choice.

Andrea shows up with a bag of groceries. Expensive ones,

with the kombucha she loves and these tiny champagne gummie candies she used to buy her on Valentine's Day. Carrie doesn't answer the door but gets her text a few hours later. The food cheers her for a couple of days. She opens the back door and stands in the sun for a few minutes. She thinks she might recover.

Then the next day it is cloudy and gray and her phone battery dies. She doesn't recharge it.

When she dies, friends from the bar write about how she inspired them to make changes in their lives. How she lived for the day. They tell stories of her singing karaoke like a real rock star, how she missed her calling as a musical theater star. They say she gave great hugs, and sent them soup and thermometers and NyQuil when they had COVID. Andrea says, She was the love of my life, without any irony, even though everyone at the funeral knew that she had said, *I'll give you two weeks to find a new place.*

For all the ways she could imagine dying at the hands of others, Carrie truly never considers that her own spirit could be the aggressor, the most heartless adversary. It's a thought she would have considered symbolic of her victim-loving generation. She thought she was different. She was tougher. She could never have imagined this slow kind of drowning in regular air, in a space that grew smaller and tighter around her, so that she eventually just didn't wake up.

THE SEX CASTLE
LUNCH BUFFET

Alix sits on a wooden bench outside the Common Café, scanning the obituary section. She blows her coffee cool, begins a slow scan of names and dates. Her therapy homework is to read every death notice and then record her anxiety using a numbered scale until her physical symptoms decrease. She's been doing it for six weeks as a cognitive behavioral exercise intended to help with her panic attacks. She initially thought she was afraid of the grocery store, the subway, crowds of hands and faces, but at the hot heart of it was a fairly mundane fear of death.

"But doesn't our mortality terrify everyone?" she'd asked her therapist.

"Not to the extent that they are no longer functional," the therapist responded.

Alix paused just as long before repeating back, "Not functional?" Alix liked to use active listening techniques on therapists, just to throw them.

She dresses well for therapy, pleated skirts and tall brown

boots. She feels ashamed of the not-functional label. It was true that before this latest exercise she'd been late filing free-lance contracts, she'd started ordering her groceries online, and she'd stopped calling her friends. All signs.

Now Alix's anxiety is in remission. She feels silly recording *zero anxiety* in the appropriate box week after week. Her therapist is pleased. That's real progress! At first, she'd read the obituaries as fast as she could, to get the task over with. Now the exercise feels like an opportunity to enjoy tiny, concise memoirs. She especially likes the old photographs. She lingers on the sentences. Today she comes across a name she recognizes: *Hiram Johnstone, 1952–2015.*

She sips her coffee, blows a kiss toward a puppy tied to a nearby bike stand, as though she has to fake being casual with herself, before turning back to his photo. Even after death, his photographed smile wanted something from the person who looked at it. The dog shifts his weight, whimpers and sits. He looks like a small bear. Hiram fucking Johnstone. She wonders if she can hug the dog. She doodles a circle in hearts and stars around his obituary, but is reluctant to read it.

Twenty years earlier, when Alix was a dancer at the Sex Castle, she spent many hours astride the pyramidical lap of Hiram Johnstone. If he'd walked by her on the street, probably even back then, he wouldn't have recognized her. To most customers, dancers only existed in three-minute intervals and then disappeared into suspended time until the next visit. Pierre, the Sex Castle DJ with the rat face and aggressive neck pimples, would cut every song off at three minutes because he

was an impatient kind of guy. It worked for the dancers, eco-
nomically, at five bucks a song.

Alix hasn't thought about that summer in years. She wishes
she were still fit enough to do side splits on a pole, but is very
happy to never have to make small talk with men as they
thrust palms full of sweaty bills toward her breasts. Even more
relieved to never have to watch them gorge on the all-you-
can-eat shrimp lunch buffet before curling a finger in her di-
rection for a private dance. Even now she shudders at the
memory of their gaping, saucy mouths, their front teeth like
high beams under the black club lights.

She stares at his photo, takes another sip of her coffee, now
lukewarm, and places her palm against her chest. She tries to
name five things around her that she can see, three that she
can feel, two she can smell or taste. A mindfulness exercise
that is supposed to prevent a panic attack, one she can feel
skirting the periphery of her body like a lion, waiting for her
to be limp enough to pounce.

At the start of the summer of 1995, Alix's first serious girlfriend kicked her out of their shared apartment. The girlfriend, whose name Alix can't even recall in this moment,
had broken her heart and moved the woman she was having
an affair with into the living room before Alix had even
packed her stuff. "This isn't non-monogamy," Alix had wailed,
"this is sadism." She overheard the ex calling her "emotionally unevolved" to the new lover. Before she left the apartment, Alix snipped all the phone wires with her nail clippers,
taped a bright red sock to the inside lip of the washing ma-

chine, and gave her girlfriend's name and address to the local Republican candidate, urging them to always put up election signs on their lawn.

She handed in her final women's studies paper, "Lesbian Fractures Within the Riot Grrrl Movement," which was basically a long diary entry with lyrical annotations, and then moved onto her friend Anna's couch. She skipped her graduation ceremony because she thought it a meaningless custom. (Now she regrets it, wishes she had a photo in cap and gown for her album.)

After that, Alix found it difficult to go to her waitressing job. She called in late, then sick, then forgot to call in. The day she finally went in, she found a new girl wearing her name tag and apron. When Alix resorted to returning bottles from the alleyway for spare change, Anna suggested that Alix join her at the Sex Castle to work a few shifts. "You could make your rent in two, maybe three shifts, tops," she said, taking a bite of an onion like an apple and sipping pickle juice from a jar. Anna sat on her long kitchen counter, wearing the one-piece pleather dress she'd fallen asleep in. Anna had perfect skin, which she swore was a result of drinking pickle juice. She said strippers made a lot of money if they used a different accent.

"My fake Scottish accent makes me the most bucks for some reason," she said.

Until that first night, Alix had a lot of stripper friends but would laugh if anyone suggested she take a swing on the pole. She was cute but not beautiful, short with small tits. Alix assumed that strippers had a kind of god-gifted femininity that Alix didn't think she could fake. But then she thought about how, if you hang out with whores, it starts to seem normal. You realize that the actresses who play sex workers on TV and in the movies are beautiful but real hoes look like almost every kind of woman. When you hang out with drug addicts, doing a line on top of your *TV Guide* after work is normal. Or when you hang out with softball dykes, suddenly waking up on Sunday to play in the park wearing ugly team T-shirts no longer seems so bizarre. If you hang out with strippers and you're stuck rolling quarters before payday to afford milk—while Anna is pulling hundreds out of her bra and sleeping in until 2 P.M.—then why not? Alix didn't have any religious or feminist hang-ups about it, so why not? That was her rationale.

"You only have a twenty-year-old ass for a year. Why not make it lucrative?" Anna asked somewhat rhetorically, handing her a pair of heels one size too big. Alix took off her sweaty combat boots and thick socks, buckled herself in and tried to stand. Anna brought out a full-length mirror, leaned it against the far living room wall and pressed Play on the cassette player. TLC's *CrazySexyCool*. Alix shook her ass in the mirror and laughed. Anna showed her how to move her knees in a way that made her ass wiggle, then squatted down and crawled across the floor dramatically, finally flopping on her back and arching.

"I call that the wounded animal crawl," she said. "Do it whenever your feet hurt. The guys love it."

The Sex Castle was not a high-end place where rich guys hosted bachelor parties. There was only a slim door at street level next to a trashy doughnut shop. There was a small sign bearing its name above the awning and that was it. You had to be told about it or notice the sign in the second-floor window. Anna had big hips and spiked purple hair and Alix had a tattoo on her back, and so the classier clubs ruled them both out. This was the nineties, when tattoos were still considered a sign of outsider status.

Construction workers came to the club on their lunch hour, alcoholics lingered away their afternoons in the front row until they fell asleep and got kicked out. Men loved the Sex Castle because they could be kings. Once you crossed the threshold of the lightbulb-bordered door at the top of the stairs, it was like stepping into 1977. Their sexist and racist jokes got laughs, their boring work stories were listened to, and they felt like the most attractive men in the world, with girls vying for their attention. No one was going to remind them who they really were.

Alix walked up the steep staircase and followed Anna, noticing how her youthful slouch shifted when she ducked through the door. Alix tried to mimic her, pulling her own shoulders back as she reached the final stair, and then stuck her tits out and adopted a side-to-side sway. The Sex Castle smelled like any other bar, beer and smoke and sweat and drugstore perfume. Alix followed Anna up to the bar to introduce herself to the manager. She tried to stand in a feminine way, which threw off her balance and forced her to grip the wooden lip of the counter.

"This is . . . Lily," Anna said. "She's over eighteen. This is Pierre."

Pierre had a throat-slash scar across his neck. He scanned her ID card and then her.

"You look much younger than you are," he said in a thick French accent. "If you can't hack it tonight, you'll have to pay me thirty bucks to leave before last call. Three song sets. Give your CDs to Pierre, the DJ. Don't shoot up." He motioned toward a greasy-looking metalhead smoking by a pair of speakers. Alix nodded, as though she wasn't completely out of her element.

"They're both named Pierre?" Alix asked Anna in a stage whisper.

"We call the DJ Little Pierre because," she said, making a motion with her pinky to indicate *small penis*.

Fucked-up things Alix learned about strip clubs that night: Despite it being the era of identity politics, the bar would only allow one Black girl to work on each shift. A woman named Tina with a brunette bob was called "the Asian girl" because she was Italian. Tampon strings glow in the black light. You can get a yeast infection from the pole. Men had eyes like tiny televisions when they watched you. It only takes one shift to make your thighs feel strong. It starts out terrifying and humiliating and then becomes normal. That process takes approximately six stage-show rotations.

The club was practically empty—it was a Tuesday night. During Alix's third rotation onstage, when she'd finally perfected one twirl around the pole without falling, her first lap dance customer walked into the bar. He looked comfortable, knew everyone, and wore the kind of business-casual clothing typical of suburban commuters, meant to be unremarkable. He patted the waitress on the ass when he ordered a drink. He was immediately transfixed by Alix as she hobbled around the small stage to the Waitresses' classic "I Know What Boys Like."

Looking back on it now, Alix realizes that she was a terrible combination of middle class, lazy, and filled with third-wave feminist mumbo-jumbo about stripping being the new road to empowerment. And while she had emerged from an average suburb, she had thousands of dollars in student loan debt, a propensity for being fired from any job, and parents who had the attitude of middle-class people without the money to lend her in a crisis. At the time, she would've said she was tough, edgy. But she wasn't the sharpest pencil in the box in terms of basic life skills. This was a time when the term *executive functioning* wasn't commonplace. The rent at her previous apartment was only $130 a month. Even in those days, that wasn't much. That's the kind of person she was. She could never just get it together.

A decade later she'd be diagnosed with ADHD, and it all would make sense, but back then she just felt kind of stupid and inadequate.

"The root of it is your anxiety. So much of your time is consumed by worrying, it exhausts you. You have trouble managing your time," her therapist had said recently.

"Maybe," Alix had responded, though inside she was worried she was just generally defective, achievement-wise. Even now, with a thriving freelance editorial business, she is haunted by the idea of ever being lazy again. It's why she insists on coming to the same café bench every morning before returning home to work, to purposefully mimic a commute to an office so that when she returns home, she can sit at her desk and be productive.

The puppy has been outside so long she begins to wonder if its owners are neglectful. She glances inside, assumes they are stuck in the long latte line. She pictures the dog in her apartment. She could get him a cute bed to put near the window. She takes a sip of her coffee and begins to read Hiram's obituary. Her pulse accelerates, her fingers tingle.

She mouths quietly:

I see a red bicycle, yellow daisies, mint gum on the pavement, rusted bike lock, lonely dog.

I feel the softness of this skirt, the smooth coffee cup, the grit of this newspaper.

I smell spring mud, car exhaust.

I taste old gum and coffee.

Alix takes three deep breaths and keeps reading.

After her sixth set onstage, Hiram approached Alix with a coupon for one free dance that they were giving out at the doughnut shop downstairs. Alix raised her eyebrows after reading the coupon.

"Uh, seriously?" Dances were five bucks a song. In those days, that wasn't much either.

The bouncer, who also had an impressive throat slash scar—did the owner meet him in a support group for failed mob-hit victims?—came over to Alix.

"You have to accept those coupons, new girl. Sorry."

Alix strode over to Hiram, took his hand, and walked him to the VIP section of the room, a dimmer area with armchairs pushed against the mirrored walls. She began to dance in front of him, worrying how she might casually and gracefully end up on his lap. She leaned in half-heartedly, looking down past his face, while climbing up to place one knee on each arm of the chair.

"You have sad eyes," he said as Alix moved above him, sweaty fingers puckered to the mirrors behind his head. She tried to mimic what she'd seen the other girls do. She was awkward. He seemed to like that she didn't know what she was doing.

"My whole family was killed in a chairlift accident," she deadpanned.

His eyes widened, annoyed at being jolted out of a fantasy. "Really, baby?"

Alix anchored both knees on either side of his lap, locking him in. "You're even more of a moron than I originally thought."

"You're a real bitch," he said, but he wasn't mad. He looked amused. "Did your daddy teach you to talk that way?"

"No, but my daddy did teach me to tip when you've had a good time," she said as the song ended, using a line Anna had given her.

Hiram reluctantly parted with five bucks. She tucked it into her G-string.

"You look way too young to be working here," he said.

"Maybe I am." She smiled. He handed her a business card. Hiram Johnstone. Talent Agent.

"Call me whenever you're working and I'll make a special trip to see you," he said.

Alix nodded, put the card into her impossibly tiny purse and whispered to Anna, who was in an acrobatic position astride a trucker.

"My first regular!"

Soon, Alix found her look. She stuffed newspaper into the toes of her shoes, ugly navy-blue pumps from the thrift store, along with a too-tight white polo shirt and a short plaid skirt that was part of Anna's old high school uniform at Mount Royal Academy. Alix still didn't know what she was doing. She'd had a lot of sex, but until she met her first girlfriend, she'd never come with another person in the room. Sex was for someone else, even before there was money exchanged, she knew this. Even when the boys were nice and had read Andrea Dworkin, it didn't matter. When Alix had sex with a girl, who pursued her harder than any boy ever had, she walked home with her panties in her knapsack feeling like, *Oh well, I guess I don't like that either.* She told people she was bi, but really, she was nothing. Until she met her first girlfriend, whom she fell in love with so intensely it altered her whole universe. She'd understood love, but desire had always seemed unnatural, until it didn't.

At the club, Anna and Alix would dance to the Ramones and Iggy Pop until the DJ rebelled and only played Def Leppard and Guns N' Roses. This was before it was cool in an ironic way to like heavy metal again. This was pure bad taste. They were above it, even though they were bad strippers. The real strippers—Anna had nicknamed them Silicon Valley—hated Alix and Anna and called them the "college bitches." Silicon Valley dated the Mafia men who came in at last call, and had physical fights over who stole another girl's tampons in the dressing room. Silicon Valley knew that Anna and Alix were in it for the story first, and then the money, while they were in it for real.

Being around naked women wasn't very sexy. Except for one girl, Lila, who would dance very slowly, slower than the song, and you'd think that would look awkward, but it didn't. It was exactly the way you should dance, except most girls were either nervous or bored or coked up, so they danced as fast as they could, trying to outrun their stage time. Not Lila. She took her time. Alix was always naked by song two, or else she wouldn't stop thinking about what she still had on, and how she was going to take it off, and what if she caught her G-string in the hook of her heel and fell? (This only happened once. Hiram brought her tissues for her scraped knee.) Anyway, by the time Lila got to her third song, you literally couldn't wait to see her pussy. It was like being denied food for days. She just knew how to hold on and smirk at you like, *What? Maybe you don't deserve it yet.* Lila always made the most money, but hardly ever took her panties off.

The only other dancer who could make as much money was Izzy, who was thirty-three. At the time, Alix thought a thirty-three-year-old was basically a senior citizen and the most pathetic thing in the world was to be a thirty-three-year-old stripper. Izzy had a mescaline face. But she raked it in.

Now Alix *is* thirty-three and she still feels seventeen, and she feels bad that she was such a jerk to Izzy, who was just trying to get by. It is easier to be kind in your thirties, she thinks. She writes that down in her anxiety journal. The dog pulls the leash as far as it will go and sits on Alix's foot, rubbing its head against her ankle. Alix loses herself in the feel of the dog's fur, petting his soft head.

Later they found out Lila was seventeen. She said she could work there because her uncle was in the Mafia. But Alix never found out if that was actually true because it was what every dancer learned to say when clients crossed a line. A whispered "My uncle Tino's in the Hells Angels" was the quickest way to make a posturing man look like a tiny little boy, returning his hands from your breasts back to his lap.

Alix's moneymaker was the fact that at twenty, she looked fourteen. Sometimes people even mistook her for twelve. Guys like Hiram Johnstone, with certain predilections for age play, flocked to her. After their first encounter, Alix went down to the phone booth in the doughnut shop, Hiram Johnstone's business card in hand, and looked him up. He was listed. It was his actual name.

The next day, Alix went to his house. What kind of a pervert moron gives a stripper his real address? Alix sat on her skateboard on the sidewalk across from his house wearing baggy pants and a toque. She smoked, read a paperback detective novel, and rolled backward and forward on the skateboard. Eventually, he drove up in a rusting Toyota Tercel hatchback.

When he got out of the car, he looked right at her but didn't recognize her. Strippers are like teachers: when you see them outside the usual context, you don't really see them. She watched him unpack groceries from the trunk and help his wife take a kid out of a car seat. An older girl, about fifteen or sixteen, got out of the car quickly and went inside, slamming the front door. His wife was beautiful. She was the kind of beautiful woman who would push ahead of Alix at the coffee shop with her big designer purse. His wife looked at Alix, who coughed on her smoke, got up, and rolled away.

As he got to know Alix, Hiram Johnstone became braver with his banter. How was school today, Lily? Did you do your spelling homework? Alix would joke that her eighteenth birthday was swell! She wasn't into it, although there she was, in a schoolgirl's uniform, giving him a little thrill.

One day he came during lunch hour and pulled her away from the bar, where she was pretending to enjoy a watered-down ginger ale and reading a class assignment, *Pussy, King of the Pirates* by Kathy Acker. "I don't like to see you reading," he said, grabbing her by the thin strap of her purse.

She began the usual banter, the regular moves. Because it was early, they were almost alone in the VIP room. Instead of sweetly asking about her day at school, participating in the ruse of an imagined high school life, he pinched her thigh and said she was getting fat, then he held her by the waist against his lap, not letting her dance.

Alix tried to go with it, rolled her eyes. "What's your deal today, Hiram? You're not usually such a grump." She lifted both arms, pretending to still be dancing with the top of her body, as her bottom half was in the vise of his arms, gripped against his bulging lap. She glanced quickly toward where security should have been standing.

He kept his hands on her waist long enough, staring at her so insistently, so murderously, even her teeth hurt from the chill. "Don't get uppity, missy. Do. What. I. Say." Then his face looked as though he was grimacing in pain. Was he having a heart attack? She wondered if she could remember the CPR instruction she'd received in junior lifeguarding. She'd never seen a man come before, only heard it in the dark, so it was a surprise to see the evidence on her skirt. When she realized it, she moved so quickly that her heel knocked his drink off the side table, causing a crash loud enough that security popped his head in. She grabbed a cocktail napkin to wipe her lap and shuddered. An inventory of diseases scrolled through her brain. She flicked the straw from her drink toward him, hoping to hit his face, but it fell flaccidly against his arm and he didn't even notice. His eyes were closed, like he was napping, and he mumbled, *Sorry, pretty baby*. She went back to the bar, shaken up. He walked by her on his way out, handed her a fifty, and said, "Here's your allowance."

The next time he came into the club and saw her, he picked out a new girl, someone younger. Alix was relieved and also annoyed.

The new girl put borage flowers in the dressing room, purple buds soaking in tap water and crowded into a plastic Pepsi cup. She snacked on them. "They're antidepressants. They used to give them to soldiers to help them be brave!" She had a tattoo of Emma Goldman on her ass, but Anna and Alix pretended she wasn't one of their own. They made fun of her with Silicon Valley because she didn't shave her bush.

One day at the bar, the new girl said, "Hiram's a fucking perv, right?"

"It's all relative," Alix had replied with a shrug. She thought about saying something more, but stopped short. When she'd told Anna about him coming, she'd laughed and said, "Gross, dude! I hope he tipped big." Alix felt embarrassed that it had seemed like such a big deal to her.

At some point, Alix just stopped going to the club, the same way she'd stopped going to her other jobs. She started working at an office, got a master's degree, and moved to another city. Anna is a lawyer now. Lila is a documentary filmmaker.

Alix finishes the obituary, learns that Hiram died of heart failure, had three grandkids. She thought about the hours she spent naked with him, legs in a V, toes pointed and touching the mirror beside his ears. Every time she did this, she had a vision of snapping his neck with her ankles, and the thought would make her worry that she was a bad person. Later, she would learn this is a common symptom of OCD, an irrational fear of hurting others when you don't actually want to hurt anyone.

She writes *zero* in the box next to the day's date in her anxiety journal, remembering Anna's advice on their first shift: "If you fake it, you'll eventually feel it, your body won't understand the difference."

Alix places palm to heart and inhales.

Brown dog. Scooter. Hipster girls holding hands.

Drip of air conditioner on my shoulder. Itchy toe.

The smell of rain approaching.

I NEED A MIRACLE

The day Stella Blue turned eighteen, she felt compelled to clean the van. Fender to bumper. This stage of pregnancy is called nesting, but Stella didn't know she was knocked up. She felt itchy. She poured vinegar onto a ripped T-shirt and rubbed the dashboard down. It was one of Matty's pink tie-dyes, and scrunched up in her fist it looked like a bloody heart.

She called her mother at dawn from a pay phone outside a Gas N' Go in rural Vermont. She couldn't remember the irritation she'd felt about her before the trip. After the beep she said, "Hi, it's Sue." She leaned back against the phone booth glass, head cushioned by a mass of bleached blond dreadlocks. She pictured her mother pulling weeds from the garden in their suburban backyard in a yellow wide-brimmed hat. "Anyway, I'm, like, sorry and shit." Her mouth tasted of metal. "You know, for leaving."

After hanging up, she pressed a long, thin sticker onto the cradle of the phone. It read: *The 1990s—A Decade for Disar-*

mament. Matty laid on the horn. She ran back to the van, ankle bracelet ringing its minuscule bells. He took off without waiting for her to buckle herself in. She wouldn't ride without a seatbelt, after seeing a woman ejected through the windshield of a small compact near Portland. When he doesn't wait, she sighs as if they've been married for thirty years. But he turns to her and says, "I've never loved anyone as much as I love you." Everyone else is asleep, but Matty is the type of guy who would say that in front of the whole group.

She fell asleep in the passenger seat and woke up when the van slowed in traffic near their destination in Stowe. Matty, Kim, and the Brain went to the parking lot outside the open-air venue, trying to procure their *miracle* tickets to the show. The Brain wrote *I Need a Miracle* on his chest in Magic Marker. They usually found free tickets this way.

Stella was alone for the first time in weeks, wasn't sure what to do. The van sat on the side of the highway ten miles outside Stowe in a line of several hundred similarly decorated vehicles. It smelled like boys, neglect, a belief that deodorant was a tool of the Man. Farts. It was a hot August day, and they'd been following the Grateful Dead since June.

She'd originally conceived of this trip as romantic. She pictured her and Matty bonding outside daily life and really solidifying their relationship. At first this drama bore out; Matty was gentle with her, showing her the ropes of being on tour, making sure she was safe. But over the weeks she'd become more closely bonded to Kim, who was nothing more than an acquaintance they'd picked up after the first concert in Buffalo. They had taken to leaving the stall doors open while they took a shit, talking as though nothing was abnormal, about who did what the night before, what song they most hoped to hear at the next show. Kim's hair was turning into a thick red scarf at the back. "I place too much of my self-worth on my hair," she said to Stella, washing her hands in the white sinks of a McDonald's bathroom somewhere in the Midwest. That was weeks ago, and even Kim was starting to grate on Stella's nerves, the way she snorted when she laughed.

Stella worried that she and Matty would become estranged, the sheen of their relationship dulling the more time they spent cooped up in close proximity. Stella was beginning to worry that she would no longer know how to be alone, or what to do if she were left somewhere without them. At the same time, it felt like her friends were gnawing at her just by exhaling too loudly. She no longer cared about seeing the Grateful Dead. She had thirty-five ticket stubs pasted into her journal made out of recycled juice boxes. They all said 1992. She didn't admit it out loud, though. The music wasn't moving her anymore. Maybe it never did. Maybe it just made her feel a part of something larger.

She shook out the smoke-soaked batik curtains, emptied the ashtrays into the ditch, wiped down the headrests with tiny lemon-scented moist towelettes stolen from a fast-food joint the Brain insisted on visiting when he was on mushrooms, yelling NO MORE TOFU! into the drive-through speaker. Stella made them eat the junk food outside the van so it wouldn't smell like meat. She spooned lumps of tofu miso stew from the cooler into a metal camping mug and ate, feeling smug. But she'd also taken a sip of the Brain's Pepsi after he fell asleep. Even though back at St. Joseph's Secondary School of the Arts she had designed pins to boycott Pepsi for their involvement in Burma. It was so cold and sweet and tasted like grade-seven pizza parties in Laura Murray's basement. She pictured Laura Murray getting ready to drive off to college about now, dragging her mother around Zellers, picking up supplies for the dorm.

———

Stella spit-shined the ubiquitous rainbow dancing-bears sticker and the glow-in-the-dark pot leaves she and the Brain had argued over. "It makes us look juvenile. We should try to promote important issues."

"Legalizing pot is an important issue. Do you know how many people are in jail for holding an ounce? It's a freedom issue." Stella tuned him out. She had just read a book about the Black Panthers and thought whining about pot was ridiculous.

She assembled the bootlegged tapes in alphabetical order in the brown plastic cases. She even organized the drugs into small ziplock baggies, laying them flat in order of size inside a hemp pencil case. Then she duct-taped it to the bottom of the front passenger seat.

The pillows and thin mattresses smelling of cum, sweat, patchouli, and patches of lentil stew aired out along the side of the highway, a lineup of porous fabric. She folded T-shirts and sweatshirts and all the brightly colored wool sweaters. She walked into the ditch and up the side, crawling under a half-assed fence to beat the pillows against a tree. A man old enough to be her father smiled at her from where he sat on the hood of his red compact car, shirtless, in loose white khaki shorts.

"You're taking care of the family, eh, sweetheart? You're good. I can see that."

Stella didn't want to smile at him, but she did. You were supposed to smile on Dead tour, you were supposed to be nice to everyone. Now the faces in every city were starting to blur and look monstrous. She could see his old-man balls against his right leg.

Before she left in June, she felt it sincerely, the love in her heart. The possibility of intentional community. She stood in the kitchen of her suburban home while her mother said, "So help me *God*, Susan—"

"STELLA. My name is STELLA now!" Susan had recently renamed herself after the title of her favorite Dead song.

"Susan, I will call the cops. I will report you missing. You are not going to throw your life away following some aged hippies who are old enough to be your grandparents. You are losing all your brain cells!"

"Mom. You are such a hypocrite. You were a hippie."

"It was different back then."

"How?"

This is where the conversation always stopped and Stella's mother said something she never wanted to ever say, variations on "Just do what I say / You'll thank me when you're older and not in jail or rehab."

Stella slung her soft-shell guitar case over her right shoulder and pulled all her hair into an embroidered beret. She undid the chain link on the door and clicked the deadbolt to the right. "I'll be out late. Matty will drive me home."

Her mother flicked on the TV that sat beside the microwave. A news story about the Somalia affair. "Make sure he doesn't drink and drive," she said, not turning to look at her. The alarm panel beeped its goodbye signal.

Outside, the neighbor kid, Jeffrey, was shooting hoops in the driveway. They didn't acknowledge each other, though in grade school they spent every day in the tree house reading comics and telling dirty jokes until dinnertime. He was her first kiss. Last week she overheard Jeffrey in the backyard with his friend Tim, who said, "I hear your neighbor is the weird girl in the hippie dresses."

"Yeah, she's a real slut. She'll do it with anyone."

"Free love and shit."

"Totally, man."

"Her boyfriend is, like, twenty-five or something."

"I bet she'd try to do it with your dad."

"Gross, dude."

"Her dad was the one that killed himself, right? In the parking lot of Blockbuster Video back in grade school?"

"Yup."

"Sad."

"Totally. He was a really nice guy."

Stella came home late that night. She was playing her acoustic guitar at an open-mic night at the campus bar in town, covers of CSNY, Michelle Shocked, the Cure. She made herself a sandwich in the kitchen, pressing layers of iceberg lettuce and tomato slices between the white bread, slicing it into two perfect triangles. The house was dark and mostly quiet as she tiptoed up to the second floor, where she planned to watch the well-worn VHS copy of *Harold and Maude* in the den. She paused outside her mother's room, a thin row of light under the door.

"I just don't know what to do, Emily. I'm starting to think I was stupid for ever wanting her, to be honest with me. Why can't my kid just keep me in the dark?"

Stella stopped chewing and leaned her ear against the door. "That's a good question, she is almost eighteen. I know. Fuck, I'm just scared of what could happen to her out there, all the drugs and no one taking care of each other."

Stella held half of the sandwich, a greasy glop of mayo on the thick carpet. She didn't bother picking it up. "I know, I know. I'm being overprotective. I remember exactly the kind of girls we were, Em. Boys were assholes back then, and they're even worse now, because they can fake it. They know how to talk nice."

Stella chewed and was about to step away when she heard her mother begin to sob. "I just wish Greg was still alive, Em. He'd know what to do. He'd tell her to stay, and she probably would."

In the morning, Stella made her mother a big bowl of oatmeal topped with almonds and banana slices. She brewed extra-strong coffee and poured it into her favorite clay mug. Her mother looked surprised when she walked into the kitchen half-dressed for work, her blouse buttoned up wrong, stockings slung over her arm.

"What's up, Susan? Buttering me up for something?"

"No, I just wanted to talk again about my trip."

"You'll miss graduation. And prom."

Stella rolled her eyes. "You realize I'm no longer a kid."

"You're naive."

"My guy friends know women are equal now. God, we have

a chick prime minister. Matty will look out for me, and I'll look out for him."

Her mother snorted. "Don't say *chick*. And we have a female Conservative prime minister. She doesn't count."

Her mother didn't know what else to say without sounding like someone she didn't recognize. Later that afternoon she left work early to buy Stella a sturdy backpack from Canadian Tire, a plastic water bottle, a camping knife, a moneybelt.

"I'm not going to Cambodia, Mom. I can carry my money in my purse."

"Just promise me you won't carry drugs across the border."

"I promise."

"And don't do any drugs that no longer resemble the plants they come from."

Stella carried her backpack and guitar out to the porch. Her mother followed with a travel first aid kit and a journal with a book of stamps slipped into the front.

They didn't talk. Instead, they shared a pinner before burying the roach in the potted geranium. Stella handed her mom the Visine. She knew her brother was due home from work and wouldn't appreciate knowing that his mother was stoned.

Matty drove up in the van and waved. "Sugar Magnolia" was playing loud enough to hear down the block. Stella's mother started to cry. "I used to really like the song. You're ruining it for me. Why can't your generation get their own subculture?"

"Bye, Mom."

"Seriously. It's kind of sad."

"I promise to call every week or so."

"I forbid you to leave," she said, unconvincingly.

"I'll be eighteen in less than two months."

"I'll cut off your money."

"I have a job." Her mother thought she babysat. Really, she sold weed, embroidered spinner dresses, and did hair wraps on girls for five bucks each.

Stella's mother turned and walked into the house, before slamming the door and pulling the kitchen curtains closed. Tim and Jeff stood in their driveway, basketball rolling toward the curb, both of them transfixed by the van.

Matty waved at them.

They continued to stare.

Stella looked at Matty, shirtless, half a cigarette in his mouth. "I'm so fucking in love with you," she said, jumping up to the driver-side window, pulling his smoke out of his mouth to kiss him.

Matty smirked. "You're my favorite girl."

Stella stopped getting high a week before her birthday. No reason, really, except she felt like she needed her life to be in order. She stopped embroidering dresses to sell in the parking lot to make their gas money. She had called home three times from roadside pay phones while everyone else dosed and danced. Her periods often stopped from the erratic eating and sleeping patterns. She simply hadn't considered the possibility of pregnancy.

Yesterday, she watched from the roof of the van as Matty hit on a girl. She had two long brown braids and was wearing a red bra under a pair of dirty overalls and no shoes. The closer they got to kissing, the more popcorn she pelted them

with. The girl giggled when she realized what she was getting
hit with. Then she caught a kernel and ate it.

"You're like a show pony," Stella said. The girl's smile faded.

"You're getting to be a real drag, baby," Matty said, putting
his arm around the girl. She had devil sticks sticking out of
the back pockets. He kissed the girl and she giggled. He
looked up at Stella sitting on the roof and she stared back.
She felt nothing. He was egging her on. He smiled, and she
identified an emotion. Disgust. She felt a little bit of revulsion
for him, especially listening to their conversation.

"We're trying to make enough dough to get to Virginia. I
hear it's gonna be wild. You got any cash, baby? Want to buy
a shirt? We're so broke, man." Then he looked up at Stella.
"She makes dresses. Wanna see 'em?" Stella didn't want to
sell this girl one of her dresses.

Matty's dad is an investment banker. His mother, a judge.
In a year, he'd have a trust fund. Matty never called home
and never seemed to have any cash. But when the van broke
down, there was a magic credit card. When he broke his arm,
international travel insurance came out of the ether.

"My parents don't know how to *be*, man." When he first
said this to Stella, outside the art room window where they
used to meet for lunch every day in grade ten, Stella felt like
finally, a kindred. Now she realized it was one of a dozen or
so ridiculous lines Matty said to girls to seem countercul-
tural.

"You're acting like a door-to-door fucking salesman," Stella
said to Matty, who shrugged.

"Tomorrow's my birthday," Stella said, and the girl smiled.
Matty concentrated on the joint he was rolling with one
hand—his party trick.

"How old are you gonna be?"

"Eighteen."

"Ah, you're a baby still."

"How old are you?"

"Twenty-three."

Stella knew right then that if she were still on Dead tour at twenty-three, she would feel like the biggest loser on earth. Imagine being twenty-three. She couldn't picture it.

"What does age matter anyway? Irrelevant. A number!" he said, as though he just birthed the theory of relativity.

Later, the girl climbed up on the roof of the van while Matty went in search of more rolling papers. "I think Matty is the sweetest man I've ever met," she said. "It seems like you guys have history, but I'm just so happy to have met him. I'm not territorial. I want to love as many people as I can this summer."

"Well, it's good to have a goal or something," Stella said, letting her cigarette burn down to her fingers without inhaling or offering it to the girl.

The next night, it rained and Matty sprung for a hotel room just for him and Stella to dry off. They washed each other's backs with the hotel shampoo, applied new Band-Aids to blisters and aloe vera to their bug bites, and watched Ren and Stimpy cartoons on TV while sharing a large pizza. Matty apologized for being dismissive, impatient. "Don't leave me," he begged, and she promised that she wouldn't. They spent the night spooning and making up and everything felt fine again, just in time for their return home.

While Matty slept in, Stella ran across the two-lane highway to the drugstore and bought a pregnancy test. She'd realized while they were having sex how heavy her breasts felt.

Matty held one with two hands and said, "Whoa." She did
the test in the hotel room bathroom, and told him over eggs
and bacon at the diner. Matty was shocked but didn't look
that fazed.

"We can take care of it," he said. "I know where to go."

"Have you gotten anyone pregnant before?"

He nodded so casually she wasn't sure how to hold herself
as she stood up and walked outside to catch her breath.

They crossed the border at Rock Forest just as the sun was
coming up, but the border guards still pulled them over, lined
them up against the wall and brought out the dogs. Thanks to
Stella's cleaning, and a midnight festival of finishing the
drugs, they were able to get into Lennoxville by dawn without
a cavity search.

Matty dropped everyone off at the house where Kim's aunt
was gone and she was house-sitting for the rest of the summer. Matty called a hospital in Lachine and made an appointment for an abortion that was going to cost about three
hundred dollars. He made everyone pool their remaining
money in an old Expos baseball cap.

Stella slept on the couch in Kim's house. Kim made her
soup, chunks of lemongrass and broccoli.

"You can't even kill a mosquito," Kim said to her when she
told her the plan.

"It's not a baby yet."

"True."

"Have you ever been pregnant?"

"Yup. Twice." She shrugged. "But I don't believe in bringing kids into this fucked-up world. It's immoral at this point in the game."

"I just don't even know what I'd do with a baby."

"Do you want to dose, then? Give the little zygote something to experience?"

Stella didn't answer. She opened her mouth, though, laid her tongue out like a panting dog for Kim to press a tab into. Kim laughed and laughed. Stella simply swallowed.

The Brain walked into the room wearing one of Kim's spinner dresses, squares of gingham and corduroy. He was six feet tall, so the dress barely covered his crotch and clung to his broad shoulders. "I can see why you ladies wear these, they are quite comfortable." He mimicked a spinning-girl move, arms akimbo, skirt in bloom as he spun. When he stopped and stared at them again, he said, "By the way, Matty took about ten hits. Just thought you should know. It's going to be a wild night."

"Is anyone staying sober?" asked Stella, starting to panic a bit.

"Well, just you, I suppose, as usual!" the Brain said, rolling his eyes. "Mommy's gotta watch the kiddies, after all!" The Brain had started calling Stella Mommy when she began to do things like clean, stay sober, and make sure everyone contributed to gas money. It was not a compliment. And because he didn't know, he didn't understand the irony or the cruelty, and it made Stella want to poison his coffee.

Somewhere around 3 A.M., with the moon fat in the sky above her, Stella made an angel shape in the grass with her arms and legs flailing. Then she decided to keep the baby. She could feel it inside her, and she didn't want it to leave.

"I'M FULL OF LOVE," she said, "or whatever," she mumbled, sitting up. Kim and the Brain sat around a campfire at the bottom of the hill in the backyard, a group of girls played guitar on the porch above. She had to find Matty. She had to tell him her new plan. She had to harness the power of her legs.

Everyone else was in the kitchen, which was so full, like they were all on the same elevator waiting to get somewhere. The smell in the kitchen was startling, like fried things, heavy grease in the air. Nobody looked right. A lot of people were strangers. She started to long for the van, for the four of them again, the static summer. Kim's snorts. The Brain farting. Even Matty, who never once relinquished control of the tape deck. Matty's smile outside the art class window. Please.

She found him by the stove, bent over with a hot knife and some hash. "Baby," she said, touching his shirt. He turned and exhaled thick smoke, smiling. "I'm going to keep it," she whispered to him. He didn't hear. The music, the crowd. "This is supposed to happen. This baby."

Matty's face turned blank. "I suppose, Stell, if it's what you want." He leaned his shirt against the hot burner, and it lit on fire. He screamed and ducked it into the sink of ice. "Fuck, Stella, fuck, I don't need this right now."

A guy offered him a shot of tequila.

Stella started peaking.

Stella had never felt so light. It was as though she was watching a movie and she was the wandering heroine, the mythic

mad girl. She watched herself in the cedar hedges that bor-
dered the farmhouses on the lane, Kim's aunt's house vibrat-
ing with teenage exertion, the other houses cold and quiet.
No cars in the driveway. Voices around her began to have
color. People appeared and were gone in a blink. The sound
of it all overwhelmed her.

Stella was used to tripping, could lock on to joy and ride
with it, could usually control the uncontrollable. But there
were no moments that night she could harness or see from a
momentary sober place.

She walked into the woodshed next door. It was empty,
smelled like a children's-book forest, calm and curious. She
walked right into Matty and gasped to recognize him. She
held out her arms. His cheekbones grew sharp. In one swift
motion, he kicked her in the gut. Once, she fell back. Twice,
for luck.

Matty pushed past her where she lay on the ground, ran
out the door of the shed, jumped into the van. The Brain was
asleep in the back, and woke up a few miles before they hit
the border.

When the Brain poked his head through the space between the driver and passenger seats and said, "Are we running away?" Matty was so startled he almost ran off the road.

―――

When Stella woke up in the morning, she was on Kim's aunt's
bed. The room was decorated in white and gingham, and the
bedspread was a rainbow quilt. Afghans hung on the walls.
Kim was half-asleep, curled in front of the door like a guard
dog, and woke when she heard Stella stirring.

Her stomach ached. Stella knew, before she felt the wetness between her legs, what had happened.

Kim helped her up. "I didn't know what to do," she said. "I'm so sorry."

"I don't remember."

"You walked into the kitchen and fell over. You were bleeding."

"I don't remember."

"You called your mother, apparently. She's coming to get you."

"I don't remember."

Stella remembered the kick, though, in a flash.

"Listen, my aunt's girlfriend is a midwife, and she lives down the road. I called her this morning and she's going to come by and look at you. She said you should go to the hospital, probably, but I told her about the drugs and stuff, so she's going to come by in a few minutes to make sure you're okay."

"Where's Matty?"

"He took off in the van. I don't know how he could possibly drive."

Stella knew then to trust the vague memory from the woodshed.

"Are you sure my mother is coming?"

"Yes, for sure. She called around seven to get directions."

"What time is it?"

"Nine."

Stella rode all the way back to Montreal without saying anything about the kick, the miscarriage. Her mother remarked that she needed to take a bath, that she looked like she'd been to war, that she was going to make her eat lots of green vegetables when they got home. Stella drank from the thermos of tea the midwife made for her, and tried not to look as if she was in too much pain. Her mom told her about cousin Lily's wedding, and the promotion at work. Stella couldn't concentrate on what she was saying. She thought her mother must have been very lonely, to be talking so much. Every once in a while she would ask her about the tour, about the concerts.

"They were pretty fun at first," was all Stella could say. "But you can only hear the songs so many times before they lose that magic.."

"So, Matty and you musta broke up, I suppose?" Stella could see her mother smile a little, and turn away.

"Something like that."

"Well, you don't have to say anything about it. I'm just glad you called. You know I'm always here for you."

"Thanks."

Her mom nodded, turned up the radio, and began to sing along loudly with "Maggie's Farm." She said, "I prefer the original version, the one by Bob Dylan."

"I thought it was Rod Stewart's song."

"Oh, no. He just covered it."

"So did the Dead."

"What happened, honey? Did something happen?"

Stella chose her words carefully. She didn't want her mother to think she couldn't take care of herself, but she also wanted to be taken care of. She contemplated *Matty kicked me. I was pregnant. Matty kicked me again, and now I'm not.*

Her mother was wearing the earring Stella made her in art

class last year, tiny hooped hearts with red stones in the middles.

"I was just homesick, and got a little too high, and needed to see you. I'm sorry if I scared you."

"No, you didn't scare me. I'm just glad you're okay."

Stella started to cry, and turned her face into the bulk of her curled-up sweater. Her mother didn't notice.

I'M STILL YOUR FAG

I wake up fetal under the red gingham quilt. I've dropped the dosage down to ten milligrams. Things seem louder, lighter and brighter. I used to have a job, a place to be every day. Now I notice the space between things. My front teeth. The stack of *Jane* magazines askew on the coffee table, the two feet of air between my open bedroom window and the one that belongs to my neighbor across the alley. I live in the first-floor apartment of a squat red-brick triplex, the kind this city was so fond of building in the 1970s. My week is made up of Sundays. On actual Sundays, I can finally relax. I press my tongue to the red fabric and expect to taste cinnamon.

It's Wednesday. In the corner, my cello sits skeletal under a layer of dust.

This is kind of a story about how I got obsessed with my neighbor. But to understand how someone might unravel like that, you need to know who I was before.

The thing about being an artist—devoting yourself to a calling, working at something that feels like a cross between a religion and the most spectacular love of your life, all those clichés—is that most people who are artists at twenty-one aren't still artists at thirty, forty, fifty. *Don't do this if you can do anything else,* a music teacher told me in my first year of university. I can't do anything else, I told him. I believed it. And over the next decade or so I was right—I got fired from every other job besides the ones that involved playing cello. Anything else I do will not save me. For a while I thought marriage would.

Six months ago, Bob's job transferred him to Dubai, and it didn't occur to him that I might come along. "This just feels right to me" was his explanation as he sawed through a tough artery in a pork chop. We were sitting in one of those new places on Ossington that served small portions of the food we ate in rural Quebec as children, covered it in shaved fennel and then charged forty dollars a plate.

"It's crazy to be a girl there," he added as I pressed a heavy fork through a hill of maple-buttered yams. "It's not safe."

I took a sip of wine. I wanted to say, Lots of women live there and you are so North American. But I didn't. I understood what he was really saying, and so I took another sip and nodded.

In the spring, we'd been trying to have a kid. I turned down an opportunity to go on tour and started watching TV in the morning instead, a stack of pregnancy tests under the bathroom sink.

When Bob left for Dubai, we sold the bungalow. I moved into an apartment building in the west end where I used to live when I was in my twenties. The neighborhood looks nothing like it used to. It's "in transition," according to the Style section of the *National Post*. Suburban girls vomit on the sidewalks outside the bar that used to be a Portuguese butcher shop. The bar is called the Meat Salon.

It is strange to be thirty-eight and surrounded by twenty-five-year-olds. Their faces are flawless, yet they look so sad. I pull the red quilt taut to the corners and put on purple leg warmers, wriggling my toes. My feet have aged faster than anything. I throw a spring jacket over the dress I was sleeping in, and I walk to a bar on the corner to apply for a job. Even though the bearded guy takes my résumé with obvious disdain, I sit and order a drink because they are playing *You Forgot It in People* and it makes me nostalgic. When the album came out, Bob—though he was called Robbie then—said, "Why can't they just end their songs eight minutes earlier? Is that too much to ask?" Bob was a repository for esoteric facts about Mudhoney and bands I'd never heard of with 2.5-minute songs. Whether he liked it or not, that record was the soundtrack of our first summer together. The bartenders played it constantly. I hummed the songs while biking home, addicted.

I had been dating girls since college, so when I met Bob, he wasn't exactly on my radar. I used to have this weird tic where I could never remember men's faces or names. We worked together at a café on Queen Street and eventually he told me that almost every shift I called him a different name. I thought there were two guys with beards and one was Eric and one was Toby, but it turns out there was just one guy named Robbie and it was Bob. We both had a crush on the bitchy redhead who wore age-inappropriate pigtails and halter tops.

It was impossible not to admire her tits in whatever she wore. She hated us both. One time she let me make out with her at a staff party, but that was as far as I got. She was nicer after that and would randomly flash me when I passed by her in the hall between the kitchen and the bar.

Every morning, I counted the till and wiped down the tables while Bob made the croissants in the basement. He started to bring me a warm one from the oven every morning. "This one is a little bit too ugly to sell," he'd say, handing it to me on a white saucer. He made me mixtapes, fixed my bike tire, brought me strange handmade jewelry crafted from garbage. I started dressing up for work, a little eyeshadow, a better shirt. He started to come to my gigs. The first time we made out, we were laughing so hard. *You know what I want to do to that bitchy redhead? This.* And then we'd act it out. At some point we forgot about trying to bang her and focused on each other. After years of getting my heart broken by a string of girls who didn't believe in monogamy, it felt nice to be chased. When you have the upper hand, it can feel intoxicating. In your twenties, anyway.

There was something so lovely and simple about dating Bob. We didn't have to talk about everything. I didn't feel like we were a straight couple, we actually felt more like two fags. Lots of sex, no processing, no rules or expectations. He kept saying, "You don't need to know where I am all the time? I don't have to meet your parents yet?" On our first anniversary he brought me a bouquet of wildflowers. The card said: *I'm still your fag.* Like the Broken Social Scene song.

I didn't even realize it was our anniversary. I spent that whole year thinking I was just having fun. Some mornings we would lie in bed and I'd tell him about girls I had crushes on,

or he'd help me write Craigslist personal ads to find a girlfriend. It wasn't a real thing, right? It didn't have archival
footage, a beginning and end. Whoever starts out beloved
ends up being the one who is left. It's simply the law of the
universe. You start out careless, just getting laid. Then you
end up throwing up rye toast in the alley behind the record
shop wondering if you'll ever love again. Or palming a box of
samples from your therapist, who suggests you need to get
back on track.

I used to wonder how my parents went from those twenty-
three-year-old hippies in their 1970s rain boots and ponchos
to forty-year-old teachers driving a secondhand Volvo and
watching *Murphy Brown* reruns at night. Now I know. For
us, it started with a sales job Bob took as a joke, and then
the job turned into something he was good at. Then he
bought a house near his brother north of the city, 'cause it
"made sense financially," and I went with him, also thinking
it was kind of a joke. An artist with a house? No one in my
generation owned a house, unless they had rich parents.
And then one Saturday we were at Walmart in suburban
Toronto, and we were almost thirty-five, and I thought, *Let's
have a kid.*

In a way, you could say I escaped the fate I probably never
wanted anyhow. Except now I'm back in the old neighborhood, ten years older and untethered. Everyone old in the
new neighborhood walks around like they paid too much ad-
mission, as though nothing has been fair since their first black
eye. The only happy faces are the visitors, the ones buying the
condos or partying in the city on the weekends, parking their
cars illegally, and pissing against my living room window while
screaming things like, "Holy! Fuckers! I love my life!" Some

live above and below me and wake me with the sounds of their experimental noise projects. They remind me of me and Bob, before we decided to grow up. On the answering machine, my mother says, "Toronto is only for ambitious people. You should move back home and start over." I press Save and make a note to call her back. Montreal does feel like an anchor, where there is less pressure to be linear. I would probably play the cello in Montreal.

And though I am unhappy, I am not as unhappy as my neighbor. Our buildings are so close together that if we both reached out our arms, we could press our fingers together. I can see through her window, even if I'm not trying. Her apartment, like splayed legs, relaxed with the assumption of no onlookers. I blush every time I see she's left a plate with half-eaten apple slices beside the bed. A cup of water turned on its side, drooling onto her dresser top. I hear her alarm every morning, and sometimes she cries, this low, rhythmic weeping like a bass line. "It's over," my neighbor says about twenty times a day into her phone.

Sometimes I wonder if I'm falling in love with her. I've never seen her face, her apartment is too shadowy. I conjure her face as angular, to fit her voice. I imagine her fingers outstretched, cupped like parentheses, around my head if I were to lean out the window. I draw sketches of her in the notebook my therapist says I should carry in my pocket.

A drug dealer named James lives in the basement apartment next door, underneath the girl. People move down the narrow alley like minnows; their arms transform into gills, calling out his name. Sometimes visitors stop to nap on the front lawn of my building, like kindergarten children on mats, restless kicking, protruding pouts. Sometimes it helps to see their suffering, because I know they are feeling a type of opiate bliss that can't compare to anything else. I've never done heroin, but Bob had, and that's how he described it. Now, when I see people on the nod in the alley, I think, *How nice for them* instead of *How sad.*

"It's over," my neighbor says, louder this time. With finality. I pretend to be cleaning my window with a discarded sock, my nose touching the screen to hear more, but she hangs up the phone. My own phone rings, startling me. I almost expect to hear her voice, but it's the bar on the corner. The bearded man tells me they need a barback on Friday nights. "Can you play the trumpet?" he asks. "Of course." It was the kind of hipster bar where the servers would randomly break into song with the house band.

Bob sends me emails and says he misses me. "Have you fucked any whores?" I write. "Have you?" he replies. It's like old times. But it doesn't feel liberating, I feel like I'm in the wrong movie, a character in some mumblecore film, only I'm the chick in the beret who serves as a warning to the hero not to go astray. I miss Bob, the way his presence made me part of something larger, but I also don't miss him at all. I make a list of his terrible qualities and tape it to the fridge.

Never cleaned the forks properly.
Kisses too slobbery.
Would get in the shower at 7:59 if we needed to be somewhere at 8:00 P.M.
Often complained about women who wrote confessional memoirs, as though their work was distasteful, but praised male memoir writers for similar work.
Starting to believe in capitalism.

On Friday night, before my first shift on the corner, I hear my neighbor on the phone. "You like that?" she says in a demanding voice. I peer through the gauzy curtain. She's got a laptop propped on her bed. She's lying back against the wall, her legs spread in an upward V. I can see a tangle of her brown hair on her shoulder, her left leg propped up. "Yeah, you better like that," she says.

I think about her all night as I serve beer the way I used to. When the other bartenders pull out their instruments, I gamely play along, metal mouthed and pitchy. I drop down to five milligrams. I can see color again.

One early morning, my neighbor's alarm goes off for half an hour. Her blinds are closed tight, no lines of light. I go to the back window and see James, the drug dealer, standing in his backyard, beside an old-fashioned barbecue. He's wearing tattered pink sweatpants and holds his head in his hands. "TURN OFF YOUR ALARM!" he yells. He looks up at my window, thinks it's my alarm since my lights are on. "It's not my alarm! It's next door!" But we are indistinguishable, the windows.

The alarm stops.

James coughs something up.

I fall back into my bed. I wonder if the alarm has a time-out function and if my unhappy neighbor has been lying there dead the entire time. I try to hear her breathing because, even though we've never met, I want her to stay alive. An hour passes. I'm almost asleep, because even five milligrams means I care only in short spurts, my hand curled gently around my baseball bat like an uninterested lover. Then I hear my neighbor cough.

Bob calls and says he's met someone. A co-worker. He's drunk, so I can barely understand him, but I take it they met before his job transfer. "I'm sorry," he says, "but she's so much like me." I don't say much. I ask, "She's straight, I guess?" Bob rarely thought about my queerness in our later years. I usually had to remind him. But he sighs heavily and says yeah, that's kind of nice about her too.

I join a text-based queer dating app called Lex. I don't know what to put for my sexual orientation. I decide on femme for butch. I could say bisexual, but I don't like the word. It conjures something I'm not. Even though my neighbor is femme. My ex is a cis guy. Butches are my original love; I would only date butches if I could find enough of them to date. At the post office an older butch in front of me in line turns to look at me and says, "Nice tattoo." I blush. "Thanks." Then she looks again. "And that's a lovely dress." I'm being read correctly, I think. *She saw me! Femme me!* I write in the journal my therapist suggested I keep to track my emotional progress. Write as though no one will ever read it. And I do.

I start sitting on my front stoop and watching the doorway of the building next door, hoping to find her. On my days off I buy six-packs and pretend to read while surveying the comings and goings. It's nice to be away from the landline so that when Bob calls, he has to leave a voicemail, maybe he'll think I've got a life again. I get a cellphone but don't send him the number. I put my cello in the back of a cab and take it to a guy I know who can restore it to what it once was.

Bob leaves me two voicemails. He misses me. He likes my ambivalence. The new girl is on the marriage track. He's

thinking of moving home. I delete them. I look at her Instagram. She makes a lot of miniature crafts. I can tell they are
broken up because she posts a photo of a cracked plate with a
cryptic sentence underneath about loss. It's the kind of vintage plate Bob would give as a gift in the courting phase. I
block them both.

It takes five days, but eventually my neighbor rides a bicycle up to the building and locks it to a rusty stand. I don't
know how I know, maybe the shape of her legs, the sound of
her voice when she says hi to one of the regular nappers on
the grass. This is my one chance. "That stand is broken," I
say. "It's hard to notice, but someone sawed the bottom so
they can steal bikes more easily."

"Thanks," she says. "Even though it's a piece of shit, I
couldn't survive without it. I work downtown, and public
transit makes me want to kill myself."

I stand up, I offer her my last can of beer. We proceed to
have ten minutes of small talk, during which I have an elabo-
rate daydream about our future together. Something about
her makes me want to hand-sew the hole in her jeans, make
her fancy salads for dinner. I come back down to earth only
when I register her saying, "That's why I'm moving to Calgary."

"Calgary, why?"

"For grad school," she says, in a way that makes it obvious
she's repeating herself.

If I have more than two beers, my short-term memory goes.

"Anyway, I should go inside. My boyfriend is waiting."

It's then I realize I've been talking to the wrong person.
She doesn't have the right legs at all, or the right hair. I wait
by the window to confirm it. No one is there. But the spell is

broken. I don't want to meet my neighbor. People are far more interesting when you don't know them.

That night at the bar, a woman I went to university with comes in and orders a gin and tonic. I've taken over for the bartender, who called in sick one too many times. "How come you don't age? Your face, it's the same," she says to me. Eventually, after four more drinks, she confesses, "I've had two kids, and my life and my body and nothing about me is my own. Don't you wish we were still twenty-five?"

I wipe the bar down in circles and offer her a smile to will her out the door. Across the room, a woman coughs, telltale. I see a strand of brown hair fall across a perfect shoulder.

MURDER AT THE ELM STREET COLLECTIVE HOUSE

I have your list of questions here, *hello?* Is the volume all right? You said to start from the beginning. I'll start from what I remember about that night. I have my old journal here. So our roommate John was dead on the floor of the living room and we were all upstairs texting each other passive-aggressively about who was responsible for leaving the air fryer on so long that it caused clumps of tempeh to stick to the metal basket. I remember that every text was normal, no signs of embellishment or unusual use of emojis. I looked over the thread again on my laptop after the cops took our phones, I didn't notice anything that seemed unusual. I printed it out, I'll email it to you. I remember thinking that Colin still couldn't spell. Wendy was the only one who used punctuation. (She wrote something like *everyone knows I don't eat mold soy turd.*) No one overexplained. Nothing that pointed to any of us knowing that his body was below us, that our cat Billy Ray Meow-rus had stepped in some blood and then wandered around the body before ripping open the bag of kibble and going to town.

Tara's only contribution was to write *you're all spoiled assholes just clean it up*. Which was how she responded to most threads in the group text. Tara had once been homeless, so no one ever told her when she hurt our feelings. I'd been living there a year but still felt a bit awkward whenever I ran into Tara in the hallway.

What was the house like? So if I had to describe the house, it was the right side of a crumbling brick duplex in Kensington Market. To the left of the front foyer was a double room—a dusty bay window overlooking the street shone strips of daylight onto a futon couch, the light never reaching the dining room behind it—a table piled high with issues of *Jacobin* magazine, art supplies, and unopened mail. The small kitchen looked out onto a yard of rusty bicycles, a haphazard garden of tomatoes and kale, a picnic table painted sky blue with burn marks and writing all over it. It wasn't artful enough to be called graffiti. The second floor had four bedrooms—Tara, me, Wendy, Colin, from front to back. There was a slim door next to the bathroom that pulled open to reveal a steep staircase to the attic where John kept an empire of vinyl records, and a mattress on the floor in the middle of the room so that he wouldn't hit his head on the slope of the ceiling when he stood up.

When we got downstairs—Tara first, and then all of us after her screams—John was obviously dead. He had an immediately visible, utterly terrifying head injury. I had never seen a dead person before, but something told me to kneel beside him so that he'd know he wasn't alone.

No one had been angry with John that week, and this was a house where no one could kill the basement rat, so we just stopped going to the basement and barricaded the staircase doors with things we'd read "rats don't like." When we told Tara our plan, she texted *rats like everything, you're all spoiled.* But what I'm trying to say is that no one was violent or had a temper. John was very soft-spoken, super sweet.

We lived collectively. We had community values, we were committed to social justice blah blah, you know. Basically, we all worked to keep the house going and before someone moved in we made sure they had, like, ethics around community care and anti-capitalism and stuff like that. Except for John, we all went to a nearby arts college where students graded themselves. At school and at home we had weekly meetings about personal responsibility, collective responsibility, humanistic principles, recycling, polyamory, and why no one should ever call the cops. But when we saw John dead, we called 911 immediately, zero hesitation. Colin was the first to get through, so the rest of us hung up. He was white as a sheet as he spoke to the dispatcher. Wendy threw up into the sink, which was already crowded with flattened almond milk cartons waiting to be rinsed. Throwing up from shock was something I thought people only did in the movies. I started to cry and held John's cold hand, as if my consoling would bring him back to life.

Tell us about everyone in the house at the time. Okay, we were all under twenty-three, well, I was twenty-four. For Wendy and Colin, it was their very first time living outside their family homes. But John was thirty-two. He'd been renting the collective house since he was twenty-one and was its longest resident. We often went to him with questions like why isn't the toilet flushing, or one time the pilot light was out and I asked if we were in danger of blowing up the house, and does vinegar actually clean things or just make them shine?

We paid him rent by sticking bills inside a manila envelope in the kitchen at the end of the month and he took it to the landlord. Rent was so cheap that once people got in the house no one wanted to leave even if you wanted to kill your roommates. Ha! I said that before realizing what I was saying.

The cops asked us a bunch of questions. Who was John's partner? He was single, we all said, but they knew that wasn't the real answer. Even though his room looked like the room of a single man—a bed with room enough for one, no top sheet, a flimsy, filthy pillow that pancaked under even the smallest head. I am not certain, but I think that every current member of the collective had slept with John in the previous six months. We told them we were all students. I think that was the first thing we said that the cops really understood.

Did John have any enemies? I don't think so. I mean, he really hated our city councillor, but the city councillor didn't really know him. Like I said, he had a lot of lovers. He had one long-term girlfriend, but she moved to France. He didn't like his family and I never met any of them even though I think they live in the city? He worked at the food co-op and everyone loved him there. They closed the store when they found out he was dead.

The cops came back a few days later to deliver our phones, but it was quite clear that they either didn't suspect us or didn't care that John was dead. Despite hating cops intellectually, a part of me, a younger part, felt like I wanted them to stay, to figure out who did it. At the time I thought, Are they really leaving us all here, together, when one of us might be a murderer? I know this is a white-girl thing to think.

That's when I stopped sleeping.

Explain how the trauma affected you. Well, I guess I started suspecting everyone. On Tuesday, I thought it was Tara. I have daily entries in my journal and I suspected everyone that week. It occurred to me while I was chopping up beets for our collective night dinner. She didn't show up for the dinner. I was holding the beets in my hand, admiring the color bleeding into my skin, and had a feeling like I just *knew* it. You know when your body tries to convince you of something with a specific looming feeling? When I first moved in, I told her I was a writer, and later that day she came into my room as I unpacked and said she also wanted to be a writer. But she said she wasn't sure what to write about. And she'd heard you should write what you know. Before I had time to interject with my opinion that this was bad advice she said, "But the only thing I really know about is murder."

She didn't say anything after that. She just stood there, looking at me, until I had to look away. She unnerved me. But later I went into her room when she was at work and saw she had a whole shelf of true crime books. Paperbacks with water-logged edges, red-and-black covers, and VHS tapes of horror movies. If that was all she read, that's probably what she meant. That she hadn't thought to clarify in the moment was perhaps just a thing she did to intimidate me. She'd been homeless after all. She probably just wanted to establish her authority on my first day in the house, despite the ACAB graffiti over the front door. I wondered if she was going to start picking us all off.

I made the borscht and put it on the stove to simmer. It was so weird to be in that kitchen, by the way. The smell of bleach and the stains on the floor that were almost gone but not quite. It was super creepy. I walked to the hardware store and bought a chain-link lock for my bedroom door. Only Colin and Tara showed up for soup, despite the communal dinner being a thing we all agreed to do every week. Our conversation was about who the murderer might be. Who had we given keys to? Who had slept here and known the back window was easy to jimmy open? Didn't the cops say there was no sign of forced entry? We spoke as though none of us could have done it, but I tried to observe everyone's facial expressions, and the way they phrased things, looking for subtle signs of deception.

I slept with my baseball bat. I emailed my mother. *I'm thinking about moving home.* She said, *Feel free to visit but we rented out your room to an international student.*

The cops didn't seem to have any leads. John was just dead. And no one really cared. It was all so confusing—on a TV show his murder would have been a big deal. In real life it seemed like people got murdered and then, if it wasn't obvious who did it, they just sort of let it drop. We didn't know how to contact the landlord to tell him that John was dead. We called everyone we knew who had lived in the house before us—who was the landlord? No one knew. Colin added alarms to the front and back doors since we couldn't change the locks. We made an agreement to guard the house. He would sleep from 9 to 1 A.M. and I'd sleep from 1 to 5 A.M.

On the night John died, the cops thought he'd fallen. I heard them talking to EMS. It was a paramedic who said the mechanism of injury didn't make sense. The cops seemed annoyed at this. They wanted it to be simple. I heard another medic say, "We can't just pretend this doesn't seem like murder because the cops want to go home."

I only stopped suspecting Tara when I went to make tea in the kitchen and saw Tara watching a nature documentary and crying. I'd never seen her cry before. She usually wore a bandanna over her head, covering a crew cut, but it was off and her hair was sticking up all over the place like a child who just got out of the bath. She wore a fleece onesie and slippers. She looked like a completely different person. I sat down on the ottoman and asked her if she'd like some tea. She said something like, "No, it's okay. I just, you know, I've never been close to someone who died before." And I didn't want to say *But you were homeless, I thought you'd seen it all,* but that's what I was thinking. She said just her grandma when she was a kid. That was something we had in common and I decided she wasn't the killer. We talked about John, about how weird it was that the cops didn't care, he was a white guy and everything and the story made the news and now it's coming up again, right, because of all the conspiracy theories online and now this podcast. A lot of the TikToks really get it wrong, like yes, we were all sleeping together at some point, but he wasn't a cult leader and we weren't afraid of him, he was just, like, a pretty hot guy and sometimes these things happened. Tara said she slept with him before she realized she was gay. He was very pretty and feminine in a way, he used to joke that he was a lot of lesbians' final man before switching teams.

Anyway, Tara and I hugged that night for the first time and before the hug ended I wasn't scared of her anymore.

So then there was a period of time where I thought it was Wendy. Because she got over it too fast. I hadn't seen her cry. She sometimes cries when she sees a beautiful bird outside.

She was back to doing her makeup tutorials on TikTok, post-ing Instagram photos from the art museum and a Boygenius concert. I snuck into her room when she was at school, look-ing for a diary or some sort of clue. Her bedroom was ex-tremely neat. So neat I began to wonder if this in itself was a sign. Aren't killers extremely organized? She had one small shelf of books, a bedside table with a drawer full of sparkly markers and a Hello Kitty vibrator. I found a notebook under her pillow, but it was just a list of three things she was grateful for every day. The day after John died she'd written *bubble tea, the stray cat let me pet it today, being alive I guess???*

I should have immediately thought it was Colin; after all, men are more likely to be murderers statistically. But you'd have to know Colin. Plus, I knew how scared he was.

Out of all of us he was the most visibly shaken up.

After four days Colin and I dragged a mattress downstairs and started sleeping in the same room for safety. I'd lie on the futon and listen to him speak all of his fears to the ceiling. "I told the cop we'd been lovers, and now I'm worried he thinks I did it because every movie about a bisexual guy is about a killer."

I countered with, "But isn't John bisexual? Aren't we all, kind of?"

On the fifth day we got an eviction notice in the mailbox. It said we hadn't paid rent in six months. The landlord was going to move his family in, which is Toronto code for I'm renovicting you. We called the cops to tell them John hadn't been paying the rent. Could that be a clue? Oh sure, said the detective, in a way that was definitely sarcastic.

That night I was struggling to fall asleep when the OCD I thought I'd conquered in the tenth grade came back in the form of a thought: What if I'd killed him and forgot? What if I was sleepwalking? What if I'd been drugged at the bar that night and had no memory of killing him? What if this was all my fault?

After a few sessions with my therapist, I was able to let these thoughts go.

We didn't fight the eviction.

So how do you feel about the new information we're sharing with you and eventually with our podcast audience? Start your answer with *Now that I know who killed him.* Okay, now that I know who killed him, I mean, I was really surprised. It was a year later and I was studying for exams in my new apartment when I got the email from you about the true crime podcast that was looking into John's death. I was so happy someone was trying to figure it out! Like we had all slept in the same house with John for months, we'd all *literally* slept with John, but none of us had any idea who he was, that he was rich, that his father owned the building and they'd been trying to kick him out for years. It's kind of crazy that your podcast figured it out before the cops. Anyway, that's my side of the story.

Oh wait, the last question. What did I learn from this experience? I guess I learned that everyone loves watching murder shows or reading mysteries or whatever but that detectives and people who are really into figuring it out like a puzzle, those people don't really exist. Like even if it's their job. No one cares as much as the people who loved the dead guy. Unless he was somebody important, I guess. I suppose I used to think everyone thought murder was a huge deal. And for some people it isn't. I guess cops see it all the time and get used to it. It's sad really. The whole thing was sad. It's nothing like *Law & Order*. And it's nothing like your podcast even. Every episode you build up this story so we want to keep listening. But if you lived through it, time didn't work that way. It was mostly the spaces in between. If I believed in jail I'd say I hoped his brother rotted there for years. John was a sweet guy, he wouldn't hurt a fly. The funny thing is, his brother is like this hippie dude, like he'd seen Phish 670 times. And John was a punk, through and through. I hope I've said some stuff you can use. I'll just stop recording now.

ACKNOWLEDGMENTS

My deepest thanks to my agent, Samantha Haywood, and my team at HarperCollins Canada, especially Janice Zawerbny and Iris Tupholme for their careful editorial attention. Thank you to everyone at Ballantine, especially my editor, Anne Speyer, for believing in this book.

Thanks to Kiara Kent, who edited the original version of "Half-Pipe" for *Hazlitt* magazine; Rosalind Porter at *Granta* magazine, who edited the first version of "Wild Failure"; Susan Safyan for editing and Zena Sharman and Ivan Coyote for publishing an early version of "A Patch of Bright Flowers" in *Persistence: All Ways Butch and Femme*, published by Arsenal Pulp; Madeline Coleman, who edited the first version of "Oh, El" in *Maisonneuve* magazine; and Michelle Tea for including "The Sex Castle Lunch Buffet" in the anthology *Sluts*.

I'm grateful to my writer friends for their years of creative companionship: Mariko, Lisa, Natalie, Matt, Courtney, Grace, Alison, Chase.

So much appreciation for Ange, Lisa, Will, Paul, Kaleb, Chelsey, Chris.

Thank you to Michelle Tea, Chase Joynt, Lynn Coady, Claudia Dey, Donovan Woods, and Catherine Hernandez for the generous cover endorsements that mean so much.

I would like to acknowledge funding support from the Ontario Arts Council and the Government of Ontario for their support. I would also like to acknowledge funding support from the Canada Council for the Arts.

ZOE WHITTALL is the author of five novels, including *The Fake*, *The Spectacular*, the Giller-shortlisted *The Best Kind of People*, the Lambda-winning *Holding Still for as Long as Possible*, and her debut, *Bottle Rocket Hearts*. She has published three collections of poetry: *The Best Ten Minutes of Your Life*, *Precordial Thump*, and *The Emily Valentine Poems*. She is also a Canadian Screen Award–winning TV and film writer, with credits on the *Baroness von Sketch Show*, *Schitt's Creek*, *Degrassi: The Next Generation*, and others.

X: @zoewhittall
Instagram: @zoe_whittall

ABOUT THE TYPE

This book was set in Goudy Old Style, a typeface designed by Frederic William Goudy (1865–1947). Goudy began his career as a bookkeeper, but devoted the rest of his life to the pursuit of "recognized quality" in a printing type.

Goudy Old Style was produced in 1914 and was an instant bestseller for the foundry. It has generous curves and smooth, even color. It is regarded as one of Goudy's finest achievements.